# The Cowboy and The Lady

Hallie called out to Steele again. "What's the big secret? What've you got to lose? Everybody wants to know. They wonder where you are, why you did it . . . where you're going. The truth about the Great American Cowboy and the world's champion horse who disappear into the sunset."

"Boy, are you full of shit. With all due respect, ma'am. And you're standing in poison sumac," he said.

She jumped. She ran out of the clump of bushes, over to the camper where he was leading Rising Star up the ramp.

"You sonofabitch!" she railed at him. "You're not getting away from me. I'll follow you! I'll turn you in. I see your license plates! I'll tell the cops, you bastard—'Wild Blue Yonder!'"

He opened the front door of his camper. "No, you won't," he said calmly. "You're going to milk this story for all it's worth. The last thing in the world you want is for me to be captured. We both know a captured horse thief ain't no story." He was in the Tioga, then gone.

COLUMBIA PICTURES AND UNIVERSAL PICTURES
present
A RAY STARK-WILDWOOD PRODUCTION

# ROBERT REDFORD
# JANE FONDA

IN A SYDNEY POLLACK FILM

# THE ELECTRIC
# HORSEMAN

co-starring

## VALERIE PERRINE
## and WILLIE NELSON

Director of Photography OWEN ROIZMAN A.S.C.
Screenplay by ROBERT GARLAND
Screen story by PAUL GAER and ROBERT GARLAND
Based on a story by SHELLY BURTON
Produced by RAY STARK
Directed by SYDNEY POLLACK

# THE ELECTRIC HORSEMAN

### by H. B. GILMOUR

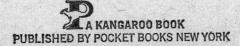
A KANGAROO BOOK
PUBLISHED BY POCKET BOOKS NEW YORK

Distributed in Canada by PaperJacks Ltd., a Licensee
of the trademarks of Simon & Schuster, a division of
Gulf+Western Corporation.

Another *Original* publication of POCKET BOOKS

POCKET BOOKS, a Simon & Schuster division of
GULF & WESTERN CORPORATION
1230 Avenue of the Americas, New York, N.Y. 10020
In Canada distributed by PaperJacks Ltd.,
330 Steelcase Road, Markham, Ontario.

ISBN: 0-671-83409-6

First Pocket Books printing December, 1979

10 9 8 7 6 5 4 3 2 1

Trademarks registered in the United States and other countries.

Printed in Canada

# THE ELECTRIC HORSEMAN

# 1.

# THE ARENA

The bull was at the top of his arc, all four feet off the ground, but Sonny Steele stayed on. He looked as if he were welded to the Brahman's back. His sandy hair whipped wildly around his leathery, tanned cheeks. His pale eyes were opened wide and there was laughter in them.

Astride two thousand pounds of mean muscle and mindless frenzy, he rode the center of the dust storm. The crowd rode with him. They cheered and stomped and felt the grit of the arena in their eyes and noses, in their gaping mouths and throats raw with acclaim.

The buzzer sounded, signaling the end of a perfect ride, but Sonny stayed on. Just for the hell of it, the fans knew. Up until now I rode for me, Sonny Steele seemed to be saying. Now I'm riding for you. Now I'm riding just for the hell of it! The crowd stood and jumped and stomped. Then Sonny vaulted off the beast, landing on the balls of his feet, with both arms raised triumphantly. And the fans were helpless with joy.

He wore his silver championship belt buckle. He brushed the dust from his hair and clothing. He brushed it off his broad shoulders and lean muscled thighs. He untied his red bandana and polished the silver buckle with it as he walked back to the chutes. An hour later, the gleaming buckle hung open across his limp body.

Two cowboys with solemn faces carried Sonny toward an ambulance just outside the arena gate. The light atop the ambulance spun. The siren screamed above the crowd's funereal murmurings. Sonny opened one eye lazily. The sight of the spinning red light seemed to incense him. He shook the vision out of his eyes. He shook the siren's mourning out of his ears. He squirmed out of the grasp of the solemn cowboys and limped back toward the arena.

By the end of the afternoon, Sonny had another silver buckle—his third. He tossed it to Charlotta, who stood in the crowd surrounding the winner's platform, and she held it up with the second silver buckle he'd won. Blonde and trim and beaming with pride, Charlotta raised the buckles for all the world to see and Sonny beamed down at her, his pale eyes matching hers for deep-down, melting pride.

Another town. Another afternoon. Another broiling sun braising beef in another dusty arena. Bulls, broncs, steers, and Sonny. Silver buckles, golden hair, and ruby-red blood.

Afterward, the cool dimness of the dressing room where Charlotta's tears sparkled like diamonds, brimming over her wide love-lost eyes, spilling down her sweet cheeks onto the six-pack of Coor's. Sonny's back was cross-hatched with red welts. Two doctors hunched like tailors over the strange fabric of skin, old scars, and shimmering new blood. Sonny's fist was white around the Coor's can as the tailors snipped and stitched.

Evening. Silhouetted against the vast purple sky, Sonny Steele raised his arms to show the crowd yet another silver buckle. Off to one side, his manager, Wendell, and his dresser, Leroy, struggled to uncork a magnum of champagne. They succeeded. Cool smoke uncoiled in the wake of the cork's festive pop. Champagne shot through the center of the smoke, soaking the stunned cowboys. Champagne arched from the wet mouth of the bottle up toward the endless sky and fell in a rain of glory onto the dusty blond hair of Sonny Steele—five times all around rodeo champion.

Sonny smiled a devastating smile, a champion's dazzling smile. His sandy mustache, his lips, and his big white teeth were wet with champagne. His tongue flicked out, to dry, to try to taste the bubbling spoils. A hard-won taste of glory. A smile full of life and mischief. Just for the hell of it!!!

## 2.

# THE SCREENING ROOM

A tight cluster of horses thundered into the home stretch. In a sudden burst of speed, Number 7, a big bay with a black mane and tail, pulled away from the pack and moved up on the outside. The crowd at the track went wild.

"Rising Star in his last race before retirement. The most spectacular stallion in the history of the turf!" The booth announcer's voice rose excitedly above the cheers of the crowd. "Triple Crown winner—with over three and a half million dollars in purses . . . he's done it! This marks his twenty-seventh win—and *what a way to go!!!*"

The screening room lights went on.

"What a horse," Bernie said in an awed whisper. He thumped the pockets of his faded denim work shirt. "Hey, Hallie, got a cigarette?"

Hallie Martin ground out the filtered stub of

the Winston she'd been smoking, took another from the pack, and handed the flip-top box to Bernie. She held the unlit cigarette between her teeth and scrawled a notation on the yellow pad attached to her clipboard.

Boyd Templeton was stretching his legs in the front row of the small screening room. "Three and a half million," he said without turning around. "Anyone know what Ampco paid for him?"

"Twelve," Hallie said distractedly. The cigarette bobbed between her clenched teeth as she continued to write.

"Jesus," Bernie murmured.

"You sure?" Templeton asked.

Hallie shrugged. "Anne?"

"Twelve million," the young researcher confirmed. "At least that's what their press release said. It's in the folder I put together for you to take to Las Vegas, Miss Martin."

Hallie tossed the clipboard onto the seat next to hers. "What else have we got?"

"Another piece of footage on the horse—a thirty-second spot . . ."

"Theirs or ours?" Hallie asked. She shook her head, declining Bernie's offer of a light.

"Theirs. It's Ampco Industries' new commercial."

"Later. What else?"

"A rodeo montage and some guest-appearance shots of their cowboy . . ."

"Sonny Steele," Templeton interrupted. "He pushes their cereals—Country Breakfast, Ranch Breakfast . . . you know, the old 'Favorite of Champions' bit."

"Well, he is a champion," the young researcher

said. She had shiny brown hair and shiny pink cheeks and eager eyes that misted easily. She was one year out of N.Y.U.'s film school and six months out of the network's training program, and the way she looked at Hallie Martin made it clear that someday she wanted to anchor a top-rated TV news show like "WBC Digest," too.

"Whose film, Anne?" Hallie asked softly.

"Some ours . . . some theirs, Miss Martin. The shots of Steele on broncs and bulls came from Ampco's publicity department. The ones where he's on his backside are ours. Oh, and there's this really strange sequence of him at a special-appearance thing. A demolition derby. The news department dug it out. It's never been aired. . . ."

Boyd Templeton took his jacket from the seat on which it lay meticulously folded. "Was," he said, standing. He slipped into the tan twill jacket that completed his conservative three-piece suit.

Hallie pushed her tinted glasses up onto her forehead and waited.

"Sonny Steele *was* a champion," Boyd said evenly. He made his way up the aisle toward her. "He's a corporate cowboy now. They own him like they own that racehorse. Hallie, I don't see a 'human interest' angle here. I'm betting that the real story is strictly financial . . . and that Ampco is going to announce it at the convention. There's some sort of merger in the wind. A biggie. That's the only angle we've got to justify this Vegas junket."

He leaned over and kissed her unruly light brown hair. "See you in first class."

Bernie stood up, too. "How come I always go tourist?"

"How come you never interviewed the Shah

and the Sheikh and the Prince and the President?"

"Because I'm a cameraman, Templeton. And that ain't chopped liver. Without me, no pictures . . . right, Hallie?"

"Come on, Bernie," Boyd Templeton said, "I'll buy you a drink."

"Right. See you in Vegas, Hallie." He took the cigarette out of her mouth and kissed her lightly on the lips. "That's what the no-smoking ads tell you to do."

"Bernie, I wasn't smoking."

"Don't stand on ceremony," the cameraman said. He stuck the cigarette behind his ear and trailed out after Templeton.

The young researcher stood beside the console at the rear of the screening room. Hallie turned to her. "Is that cowboy stuff worth looking at?" she asked.

"I think so."

"Why?"

The girl's face flushed red. She shrugged her shoulders and began to toy with the pencil attached to her clipboard. The back of the clipboard, like Hallie's, was stenciled: WBC DIGEST. The girl, like Hallie, was wearing a silky tailored blouse and soft wool skirt over an expensive-looking pair of high-heeled boots. She had, like Hallie, a luminous face and eager eyes, but not the lean, hungry edge, the purring electricity, that was Hallie Martin's trademark.

"Why?" Hallie repeated, studying the girl. "What's this piece of film going to tell us about Ampco Industries? Is there a story in their 'corporate cowboy'? Or their retired champion racehorse? Or their movies or their golf balls or their

cereals, or, God help us, their 'leisure wear' . . . ?"
The young researcher was raptly attentive now,
caught up in the shaping of a story. Hallie could
practically see Emmys glistening in the girl's eyes,
hear her ambitious young mind composing a
Pulitzer Prize acceptance speech.

She smiled. Ambition was one thing. They
shared that. But awards . . . rewards? It was hard
to tell whether the kid had the instinct to match
her drive or the stamina to track her dreams.
Hallie had been in the business for—was it possible?—almost ten years now. She must have been
just about that age, Anne's age, she thought, when
she'd started out as Les Charles' research assistant and "Gal Friday."

That's what they called it then. Women were
Gals; Gal Fridays were underpaid go-fors. Go for
the coffee; go for the wife's anniversary gift; go
for the props—an aesthetically "correct" flower
arrangement to add life to the static set; a Jensen
water carafe to look serious sitting on the news
desk . . . Someone to tie the celeb's tie; come up
with a *bon mot* for the anchorman; get the
weather maps in sequence for the juiced-up fore-
caster; make sure the ex-jock who did the sports
had a shirt on—preferably glare-resistant pale
blue—under his WBC blazer, by air time.

She'd done the dirty work and she'd pretended
that the arduous research and story verification
and instant editing of air-ready scripts for reporters earning ten times her salary and one hundred times the glory was nothing . . . a job that
any pretty lackev who preferred doing the bunny
dip at a prestigious network, instead of the local
Playboy Club, would have done . . . just for the
hell of it!

Five years behind the scenes; then five years of prying open the door to notoriety; interviewing, playing straight man to the stars; getting them to tell Hallie Martin what they didn't dare tell anyone else, not even themselves. Big deal. Five years behind the scenes; five years in the limelight, and —out of the three TV news awards possible—the score was still: no Emmy, no Peabody, no George F. Polk. Not yet!

Hallie drew out another cigarette and bit down on it. "Or is Boyd right?" she mused aloud. "No human interest here, just a financial saga about a mega-corporation . . . ? Slight sci-fi angle, maybe?—AMPCO: the Industrial Giant That Ate the World . . . that sort of thing."

The girl laughed. Hallie tapped the armrest of her seat with her fingernails. She had an appointment for a manicure tomorrow. She'd made it especially for the upcoming Ampco convention. Experience bred second nature. Second nature said: tidy up for this outing, kiddo. Corporate types liked everything to look well-tended, groomed. It didn't matter whether there was dirt under your fingernails—or under their rugs—as long as the dirt was attractively covered up.

Of course, some people actually preferred to be interviewed by someone with raggedy nails, Hallie had discovered. It made them feel superior, in control, or simply at home. Individualists did— brilliant, eccentric, neurotic, or any combination thereof—but never, never a political, military, or corporate type. Never. So she tapped her soon-to-be manicured fingernails on the armrest and gazed at the clipboard lying on the seat beside her as she recited aloud:

"Ampco General Films, Ampco Foods, Ampco

Sporting Gear, Ampco Fabrics, Ampco Automotive . . ."

"It's the demolition-derby stuff," Anne, the researcher, blurted suddenly.

Hallie smiled. "What about it?"

"I'm not sure. It's . . . he wears lights, Miss Martin. Sonny Steele—he wears hundreds of tiny little colored lights . . . like a Christmas tree or a flashing sign. There's something wrong about it. He rides into the spotlight on a horse that's all lit up, too—"

"Rising Star? Does he . . . what's-his-name . . . Steele—does he ride in on their racehorse? Or Rising Star?"

"No. Another horse. And he holds up a giant cereal box that lights up. I can't explain it exactly. There's just something *off* about it all. I mean, the man is a champion! He was five times all-around rodeo champion. Wait till you see the shots of him riding and roping and all that stuff. And then you see him all wired up, riding around that track, holding a box of breakfast cereal. It's . . . tacky. It's, well, Miss Martin, it's just not right."

Hallie ran a hand through her thick hair. Tomorrow, the shoulder-length mass would be fashionably cropped and styled—fifty dollars' worth of carefully "casual" styling—because it was going to be corporate-type time in Vegas and she wasn't about to let some fading Nevada showgirl with a beauty school diploma hack away at the crowning glory. She stared at the young researcher. It was just possible that the girl had an idea—some fresh notion of what might be an interesting sidelight to the Ampco segment of "WBC Digest." Templeton could concentrate on the corporate end. Get the financial facts and figures together. But maybe there was an angle here for Hallie to explore.

*Ex-Champ Turns Twinkling Ampco Ad . . . Subduer of Bucking Broncs Subdued by Big Bucks . . .*

"Okay, let's see it." She snapped her tinted glasses down again and picked up her pen and clipboard. *Sonny Steele—The Electric Horseman . . .* She liked that. "Anne," she called as the girl switched off the light, "call me Hallie, okay?" She slid down in her seat and faced the screen. She sat, smiling and waiting in the darkness. The unlit cigarette bobbed between her teeth.

## 3.

# THE ELECTRIC HORSEMAN

The Ampco man checked his watch impatiently. He wore a mustard-colored blazer. A corporate logo featuring a running horse was emblazoned above his heart. He stood on the ramp between the stadium and the dressing rooms. His eyes darted constantly from the huge outdoor lights in whose glow hundreds of frenzied bugs circled, to the luminescent face of his digital watch, to the dim passageway under the stands where Sonny Steele was supposed to be ready and waiting.

Somewhere under the lights two cars crashed. Applause followed the metallic din. And the incessant revving of engines gave way to the static of the track's P.A. system.

"Looks like Floyd Gerber has had it for the night!"

The loudspeakers were mounted beneath the

lights and the announcer's crackling excitement seemed to fluster the circling bugs. They broke rank as he continued.

"That means that Lester Crosley of Santa Rosa has won the Demolition Derby!" More applause accompanied the sound of a crippled car leaving the track. "And now, folks, while we get ready for the next race, we've got a special treat for you. . . ."

Behind the Ampco man, a dressing-room door opened and two men in Western gear manhandled the rag-doll figure of Sonny Steele out the door.

"Is he going to make it?" The man in the mustard-colored blazer didn't bother concealing his disgust.

"Don't he always?" one of the men, an aging dirt-hard cowboy, answered.

"Don't pay him no mind," the other whispered to Sonny.

"Forget it, Leroy. He probably can't hear you, anyways."

". . . you're going to meet one of the all-time great cowboys—" The announcer's voice rose in an attempt to capture the attention of the audience, most of whom were standing and stretching or whistling for the beer and hot dog vendors who moved through the stands. "Yes, one of the all-time greats! Five times *all-around* World Champion . . . Sonny Steele!"

The lights inside the stadium dimmed to black. The noise dimmed to an expectant murmur. Nothing happened.

"SONNY STEELE!!" The announcer tried again after a pause.

Still nothing. The Ampco man was whirling

like a dervish now, around and around, from the darkened stadium to the dim ramp. "Shit," he muttered. "Where is he . . . ? Where the hell is he?!"

The sound of hoofbeats echoed through the dark arena. The crowd quieted. The Ampco man squinted toward the center of the track. Suddenly Sonny Steele lit up. Hundreds of tiny light bulbs attached to the green and purple cowboy suit he wore flashed on, illuminating him in a twinkling rainbow glow.

The crowd cheered. The announcer announced: "Sonny Steele appears tonight through the courtesy of Country Breakfast, a division of Ampco Industries." The Ampco man shook his head and cursed quietly, an obscene litany of relief. And Sonny made a triumphal circle around the track, stopping in front of the announcer's booth to rear his horse and lift, for all the world to see, the oversized light-up cereal box he held.

"Smile, you bastard," the Ampco man muttered. "Smile, you dumb son-of-a-bitch!"

The dazzling smile full of life and mischief stared back at him from supermarket shelves and billboards and magazine ads. About the only place he never saw it anymore was in the mirror. Sonny splashed cold water on his tired face. He blinked his eyes and shook his head and willed himself back to consciousness. He'd fallen asleep on one of the molded-plastic chairs in the airline terminal. Now his back was cramping again and his butt tingled from lack of circulation. He wasn't even sure which city he was in. All the terminals had the same seats, rows of molded plastic, alternating turquoise and orange.

The door to the men's room opened and Leroy stuck his head in. "Ah, there you are, Champ." He looked relieved. "Ready? We got to do Santa Paula."

Sonny nodded his head. It thumped mercilessly. His brain felt like a knot of congealed grits floating in syrup. Leroy came to his aid. "Just lean on me, Champ. Come on, now. I got you." The tall young cowboy took Sonny's weight onto his shoulder and walked him gingerly to the door.

Wendell was waiting at the security checkpoint. His face clouded over when he saw Leroy half-dragging, half-coaxing Sonny toward the departure area.

"Where was he, at the bar?" Wendell asked as Sonny moved through the metal detector.

"Naw," Leroy said. "He was just rinsing his face. He was over to the men's room."

"Oh. Hi, there!" The girl who ran the luggage X ray smiled up at Sonny. "Saw you on Mike Douglas last night!"

She was young and pretty, with pert breasts that pressed against the bodice of her uniform. Her blouse was opened one button too low and he could see that she wore some sort of push-up brassiere. He was very tired. Her hair was very neat. He wondered if she wore rollers to bed. He wondered if her breasts were flat without the lacy push-up bra. It occurred to him that it'd been quite a while since he'd slept with a woman who wore rollers. Charlotta had, long ago. She'd stopped after they were married. He was tired and he thought that if he spent the night with the luggage X-ray girl, she'd probably pretend that she never wore rollers. And if he spent the week with her, he'd probably wake up holding a plastic-headed flat-chested woman.

He touched the brim of his Stetson dutifully and moved on. She was young. Probably she used one of those hot-air blowguns, he decided.

"Honest," Leroy said. Wendell was in his fifties, still hard-bodied with wind-leathered skin backing his full gray beard and pale blue eyes that took in more than they gave out. He was watching Sonny hobble toward the gate. He'd said nothing nor moved a muscle on his face, but Leroy could practically smell the skepticism oozing from him. "He ain't had a drink this morning, Wendell. He's just tired. All this flying and riding and waving and signing them pictures every single day and doing this radio show and that television show . . . it's wearing, Wendell. He's a good boy. He's just wore out."

"Next," the X-ray girl called and, stone-faced and silent, Wendell walked through the metal detector trellis.

By nightfall, they were in another city, in another dressing room under another stadium. Sonny was sprawled in a chair while Leroy struggled to get boots on him. He was wearing a pair of orange and blue trousers. Wires hung loosely from the waistband of the gaudy pants. Some of the wires snaked up his bare chest, resting on the scar tissue of better days.

"I can't do it, Wendell, him laying down."

Wendell had been pacing behind Sonny. He stopped now and helped Leroy haul Sonny to his feet. Together they managed to fasten the complicated back support that Sonny wore under his fringed orange and blue shirt. But the second they let go of him, Sonny started to slump back toward the chair.

"No, you don't, son," Wendell said gently. "Later."

Outside the dressing room, the Ampco man checked his digital watch impatiently. He hoped the cowboy's manager had cautioned him to ride around the *outside* of the diamond. The Little League playoffs were still in progress, and the ball park manager had told him that, Sonny Steele or not, he didn't want the kids sliding around in horse shit after the Champ's appearance.

The Ampco man hoped Steele would honor them all with a smile tonight. And that he'd try not to lose his balance when the horse reared. And that he'd remember that it was the Ranch Breakfast he was pushing tonight, not Country Breakfast . . . and that someone would remember to check the batteries in the cereal box.

The stadium lights dimmed. Sonny trotted past him in the dark. "Hixson," the Ampco man said to Wendell, "he's got to be on that plane in exactly one hour."

They traveled first class. It didn't matter much, Wendell thought. Sonny'd have slept just as well in the baggage compartment. Better, maybe. There was no drink cart rolling through the baggage belly every ten minutes and no stewardesses squealing, "Oh, don't I know you?," and no three-piece suits waking him up to autograph a cocktail napkin for Little Johnny Junior.

Across the way from Wendell, Sonny was slumped in his seat, hat over his eyes. The drink cart was rattling toward him. It slowed. From under the brim of his hat, he could see Wendell signaling the stewardess not to stop. Sonny shifted his weight and let his hand fall over the armrest into the aisle. The cart moved on. Wendell looked relieved. Sonny closed his calloused hand around the two tequila miniatures he'd grabbed.

He drank them in the bathroom half-an-hour later while he was changing into another clown suit that some costume designer had spangled and fringed. Leroy said he could change in the back of the limousine on the way to the shopping center, but Sonny said no, he'd rather be ready ahead of time so he wouldn't have to listen to the local Ampco man piss and moan. But he felt ridiculous as he walked back to his seat. Not even the dark glasses he wore helped. He'd have had to be deaf, not blind, to ignore the giggles that followed in his wake.

As it turned out, the Ampco man pissed and moaned, anyway. The shopping center turned out to be two hours' drive from the airport, and the nervous nelly in the mustard-colored blazer who picked them up in a limo decked out to look like a Ranch Breakfast box said that the costume would be ruined by the time they got there.

"He's wrinkling," the man complained to Leroy. "Look, there are spangles all over the seat! He was supposed to change in the trailer!"

They did two supermarkets that day, one inside and one out. For the outdoor "event," Sonny stood on a platform covered with AstroTurf in the parking lot of a shopping mall. He stood between two ten-foot boxes of Country Breakfast. An arched trellis over the platform was hung with a sign that said: COUNTRY BREAKFAST AND SONNY STEELE—TWO WORLD CHAMPIONS!

He couldn't remember the lines he was supposed to memorize in the limousine. He passed out miniature boxes of cereal to the crowd and ad-libbed, with Wendell's help, some sort of gibberish about how many different ways Country Breakfast helped "grow you." He was working against the noises of the traffic jam his presence had created in the parking lot, and half the time he said Ranch Breakfast when he was supposed to say Country.

The second supermarket was the Ranch Breakfast one. It was the store's grand opening and he was the main attraction. Huge displays and advertisements featuring Sonny Steele flashing his champion's dazzling smile looked down on aisles jammed with shoppers. At the front of the store, near a bank of check-out counters, Sonny stood beside the little mechanical horse the Ampco man wanted him to ride. He managed to stay on his feet for a couple of minutes while he recited the virtues of Ranch Breakfast, or tried to, into the microphone they'd set up for him.

"Why, it's better than orange juice, toast, bacon . . . toast . . . bacon . . ."

"Eggs," Wendell whispered to him.

"Eggs," Sonny said. "Better than eggs and toast and bacon and eggs, ah . . . and chicken and waffles and meat loaf and fish and olives . . ."

They turned off the P.A. system and he climbed onto the little horse.

"Hi! Lucinda. Lucinda Fairlee—The J.B. Ranch Trick Cowgirl rider. Remember me?"

A pretty girl dressed in, Western clothes waved to him from the edge of the crowd.

"Sure," Sonny lied. "Hi-ya, Lucinda."

She laughed delightedly. "Since you seen us, I'm the only original J.B. Ranch Trick Cowgirl left. All the others quit. April and Gretchen married brothers."

He looked past her, wishing he were somewhere else.

"You don't remember, do you?" she continued. "Last year . . . ? After the Watsonville rodeo?" She winked. She didn't have to. The tone of her voice alone was enough to make some of the mothers in the crowd frown and drag their children away. The Ampco man turned beet-red. He looked as though he were going to jump Lucinda —for all the wrong reasons.

"How could I forget?" Sonny said. "Lucinda Fairlee. Are you kiddin' . . . the Watsonville rodeo."

Leroy flipped the switch and the machine began its parody of a horse. Sonny bobbed up and down, up and down, in the supermarket window.

They escaped, Sonny, Wendell, and Leroy, later that afternoon. While the Ampco man and the supermarket manager pored over an order form, they borrowed the limousine and headed out to a café on the opposite side of town, the older section where there were no shopping malls or supermarkets. They sat in the cool dimness of the café, drinking beer and watching the TV set over the bar.

"Look a' that," Leroy said, as a magnificent thoroughbred stallion appeared on screen. The horse cantered in a green, sun-dappled meadow. Then, suddenly, he was traveling through an immaculate scientific laboratory.

"In research . . ." the announcer said portentously.

Wendell groaned. Leroy pulled his hat down over his eyes. Sonny stared, transfixed, as the beautiful animal galloped past an oil-drilling rig.

"In exploration . . . !" The stallion galloped past an assembly line. "In industry . . ."

"My God, what a horse," Sonny murmured.

". . . and nutrition," the announcer continued as the big bay moved past shelves full of food products.

"That's him, ain't it? Got to be."

"Got to be," Wendell agreed.

The stallion leaped a high fence. The image on screen froze in the middle of his jump, caught him in mid-air, rearing majestically. "Ampco Industries," said the announcer. "The Rising Star for a better world today . . . and tomorrow!"

"Rising Star, all right," Leroy said. "Won my rent off *that* sucker plenty o' times."

"Horse should be at stud," said Wendell.

Sonny poured himself another beer from the frosty pitcher on the table. "We all should," he said.

The Ampco man found them. They saw him paying a cab driver outside the café. He wore his mustard-colored blazer with the image of a rearing horse over his heart. Wendell stood up as he entered the café. "We know, Junior," he said. "We know."

They saw the commercial again, later that night.

They were in their hotel suite—another hotel suite, interchangeable with, indistinguishable from, any of the suites in which they'd spent a night on the Southwest swing of their tour. Nice places. Expensive as hell. Two double beds in the bedroom; color TV in the sitting room; bathroom with a paper ribbon across the toilet seat and two tissue-wrapped glasses sitting upside down on the sink. Between the TV set and the couch, a room-service cart held the tequila, bourbon, beer, bags of taco chips and bar nuts, and two Styrofoam ice buckets to supplement the little silver one that wouldn't hold enough to pack a rotten tooth. And, always, a little imitation fruitwood writing desk in the corner with one drawer full of hotel stationery so that you could find out where you were staying, if you cared.

Wendell was at the desk writing out postcards. Sonny was sprawled across the couch chasing down his Jack Daniels with beer. Leroy leaned half out of the little chair near the television set to change the channel.

"There he is again," he said when the Ampco commercial came on.

Wendell turned from the desk. His face lit up with admiration at the sight of the galloping thoroughbred. "That's the little beauty that you're going to ride in Vegas on Friday."

"That old boy's a champion. Born to win. No two ways about that!"

"Ride him?" Leroy snorted derisively and leaned back into the knubbly cushioned chair. "Not necessarily 'ride' . . . he's going to sit up on him on a stage. . . . They'll probably have rubber booties on his hooves, too."

Wendell shot him a shut-up glance, but Sonny was staring at the screen and appeared not to have heard. "Born to win," he repeated quietly. "Born and bred a champion."

"Probably had the best of everything," Leroy ventured.

"Probably never drew a free breath yet," Sonny said.

"Sign that." Wendell carried a postcard over to

the couch. "It's to Wilkin's boy. He drew Little Venus in Fairview. We've got to send him a little luck."

Sonny sat up, wincing at the pain in his back. Rodeo wounds; souvenirs. "He'll need it," he said, signing the card. "Ain't he the kid that fell out of the barber chair?"

"You stayed on *worse* than Little Venus," Leroy said.

Wendell picked up a newspaper and began to scan it. "*Ain't* no worse than Little Venus."

"Bubbles was worse than Venus. Sonny did eight on Bubbles. Nobody done him since!"

"Well, I ain't on Bubbles no more! Don't intend to be. Don't you ever get tired of going on about 'done, done, was, was'?! Isn't there one way in this world I can get you to see that them days is gone, and good riddance!"

Leroy glanced at Wendell. Then he said to Sonny, "Hell, I was just complimenting you."

"I don't need compliments right now, Lee. Get me a couple of them gorilla biscuits, will you?"

"I've got the brace, if your back's hurting."

"Leroy," Sonny said quietly, "just give me the pills."

"You already took uppers . . ."

"I don't need no mama, Leroy."

Reluctantly, the tall young cowboy stood and went to the bedroom to get the vial of pain-killers.

"Want to remember the past?" Sonny called after him. "Just about every bone in my body's got full recall. I got souvenirs a-plenty."

Leroy returned with the pills. "You also got this." He was holding Sonny's silver championship belt buckle. He handed him two yellow capsules. Sonny knocked them back with bourbon.

"Shouldn't be mixing them like that," Wendell said. "Hey, look here." He folded back the paper. "Ranch for sale in Bailey. Four hundred fifty acres."

"Bailey?"

"You remember," Leroy grumbled, "that's where you rode those real horses."

"How many acres?" Sonny asked Wendell.

"Four hundred fifty."

Leroy popped open a beer. "Wish you'd bought that ranch in Spanish Fork instead of that Malibu place."

"I don't remember you minding that Malibu house so much. You were in the water half the time, with flippers on your feet . . . like a damn penguin." Sonny smiled, but it wouldn't hold. Even his face muscles felt sore today. Save it for the supermarkets, he told himself and let the smile slide. "What the hell's the matter with you kickers? We're not on the bean-and-bacon circuit no more! You got room service. You got ladies in the lobby. You fly first class. The laundry comes back with tissue paper in it. Hell, we're living like a bunch of fat oil men. Living better than we've got a right to."

Leroy shook his head slowly. "Cowboys in the ocean? It don't make sense."

"Beats going to work every night and having a bull tap-dance on my back, doesn't it?"

"Leroy," Wendell said, "take them pants out and get them pressed. . . ."

"Beats having your legs braided. . . ." Sonny took another hit of bourbon. "Beats having your shoulders pulled out of their sockets . . . having a bull run the length of your spine using your head for a floor mat . . . don't it?"

He got up and walked unsteadily to the room-service cart. He poured himself another tall glass of Jack Daniels and shook his head. "No, it don't," he said very quietly.

Wendell started singing: "Mama, don't let your babies grow up to be cowboys!!" He poked Leroy, who chug-a-lugged the rest of his beer, crushed the can in one hand, and joined in loudly.

Sonny turned and stared at them. A grin crept over his tired face, lifting the corners of his thick mustache. He shook his head again. Then he started singing along with them.

"No, Mama," he improvised, "don't you let them . . . don't you do it . . . don't you dare . . ."

# 4.

# UNFINISHED BUSINESS

The mail was waiting in front of her door. There were only two apartments per floor and the elevator opened onto the stylish vestibule that she shared with Morgan St. James and her sometime live-in lover, Claude. Hallie had never been able to figure out from Morgan's breathless monologues just what it was Claude did, only that he apparently did it well enough to satisfy Morgan . . . at least three nights a week.

Not tonight, however, she noted as she bent to retrieve her mail. Tonight Morgan had her Claude-less doormat out. It was an unusual little rug, bordered in fragile pastel shades and bearing a needlepointed message in the middle: "You've got to kiss a lot of frogs before you find a prince."

Hallie smiled and unlocked her own door. She riffled through the letters and postcards as she walked down the long corridor toward the living room. The walls of the corridor were lined with spotlit photographs of old friends, new acquaintances, and that twilight zone between the two—celebrities whom she'd interviewed.

She took pride in the fact that all the photographs had been given to her; she had not solicited them. They were candid shots, and she liked that. No studio or publicity stills. There were some that had been taken during the taping of a show and included her, looking absurdly serious or laughing aloud or with her mouth agape in the middle of a sentence or in the middle of a yawn.

She changed the pictures occasionally. Some had been up for ages. Others were as new as last week's whim. Down near the living room was the photograph someone had taken during her first date with Roger. It wasn't exactly their first date. It was their first meeting. It was at a publishing party for his book, one of his books—she'd forgotten which one: *Crisis in Dehli, Famine at Watergate, Scandal in Pittsburgh*—some nifty Pulitzer Prize candidate or other. Anyway, Roger looked very dear in the photo. Terribly professorial, dashing, and serious. And he was frowning solemnly as he peered down the front of her low-cut dress.

He'd begged her to take down the picture. He'd tried every sort of bribery—even a proposal of marriage one very drunken night when three waiters from Elaine's slid him, like an unclaimed corpse, head first into the back seat of a cab. She'd refused, for two years now, innumerable requests to get rid of the damned picture and two more proposals—providing she'd sign a pre-nuptial agreement to destroy the print.

Sometimes she thought that what Roger did was as difficult to pin down as what Morgan's Claude did. Roger was an author, journalist, sometime presidential advisor, full-time political gadfly, and favorite commencement speaker of the Seven Sisters' college circuit. He was very tall and very articulate and very distinguished looking—most of the time. She liked him best, however, when he was being stuffed into cabs or sliding under tables at elegant dinner parties or cocking his head with intense interest at some pompous ass holding court; cocking his head, looking very involved, and then, suddenly, snoring loudly right in the boor's face.

The problem was she didn't love Roger. It was a minor problem. She liked him very much. She thought he was a good man, bright, attractive, kind, and a surprisingly hot number in the sack. He didn't like being called a hot number. There was another thing that pleased her about Roger. He traveled even more than she did. So, sometimes she didn't see him for months and sometimes they'd meet for a quickie in Kuwait. It kept life interesting. It kept life alive.

There were two postcards and a tape recording from Roger in the day's mail. Hallie tossed her attaché case onto the couch and pulled off one of her boots while she read the cards. The telephone rang before she got to her second boot. She hopped across the room to answer it.

"Hallie? Don't hate me," Les said.

"Whatever happened to 'hello'?"

Les Charles was WBC's news director, Hallie's first employer at the network, one of her dearest friends, biggest fans, and still her boss. "I gave your home number out," he said.

She sat down on the parquet floor and tugged on her boot. She told herself she needed to sit down to get the boot off. She knew she was kidding herself. She had to sit down fast, on the floor, anywhere, because intuition told her what was coming next.

"To who?" she asked.

"Brandy Harris."

Her adrenaline was anticipating. Cool it, kiddo. Brandy Harris has five hundred clients, she told her hysterical bloodstream. Save the adrenaline. Don't you know there's an energy crisis going on?

"What did Brandy Harris want with my *private*, unlisted, home number, Les?"

"Hallie, I'm sorry. I thought it had something to do with the Ampco convention . . ."

"And it did, right?"

"Indirectly."

"Les, I think my nerves are going to run out before my twenty questions do!"

"Bud Broderick asked Brandy to get your number. He conned her. Said it was an emergency . . ."

"And she conned you . . . and now what?! She didn't happen to say what the S.O.B. wanted, did she?"

"Well . . ."

"Hey, Les, my Libriums are in the bathroom, and the phone cord just isn't that long! Twenty questions again? Bud Broderick, star of Ampco Films' new epic, is going to be in Vegas tomorrow, right?"

"Right."

"I read the press release. . . . Hold on, you . . ." She put the phone down and rolled toward her purse. "Asshole!" she whispered fiercely. She dragged the purse over to the phone and rum-

maged in it for a cigarette while she continued.
"Okay. What does he want with my number?"

"Hallie, don't hate me . . ."

"You're redundant. What, Les?! What the hell
does that . . ." There was a click on the line. "Oh,
Christ. Another call. Can you hold?" She hit the
button. "Hello?!"

"Still mad at me?"

"Hold on!" she barked. She pressed the button
again. "Guess who?" she said to Les. "I'll talk to
you later." She disconnected Les Charles and hit
the button for Bud Broderick's call.

"What do you want?"

"You're so . . . direct, Hallie. I guess that's what
makes you such a terrific interviewer."

She bit down hard on the cigarette.

"Hallie . . . it's been a long time. Too long."

"Oh, you know how it is, Bud. Time flies when
you're having fun."

"I never miss your show."

Oh, Christ, she was crying. She couldn't believe
it. Three years after the fact—tears! She sniffled
loudly.

"Darling," he said, "are you all right?"

That did it—the honeyed condescension dripping from his lying lips. He had hair on his shoulders, she reminded herself. He snored. The little
toe on his left foot crossed over the toe next to it.
Hallie Martin stood up. She even bothered to
brush the wrinkles from her soft wool skirt. She
pushed her hair back from her flushed face.

"Bud," she said, "cut the crap. I don't like you.
Did I ever mention that?" She could hear his sudden intake of breath. "I don't like you. I don't trust
you. What do you want?"

"A fair shake," he said.

She almost laughed. "I know you're not going to believe this, pal," she said, "but I don't know what the hell you're talking about!"

"You're going to be in Las Vegas . . . at the Ampco convention, right?"

"Right. And so are you. They're going to be showing off everything they've got for sale . . ."

"I've got to do a press conference for them, Hallie. You know they produced my last picture. I'm going to be up on that platform, and you're going to be out there asking the questions. I want you to go easy on me. I want bygones to be bygones . . ."

"Did you really think I'd wash your dirty linen in public? I didn't enjoy the job that much when I was doing it privately, if you recall."

"Hallie . . . I'm sorry."

"Bud . . . you're a liar."

She hung up, pulled off her other boot, and walked directly to the bathroom. She washed her hands, sudsing them lavishly, rinsing them with ice-cold water, and soaping them again. Then she began to laugh.

She'd read Freud. She knew what all this compulsive hand-washing stuff was about—guilt. That's what Siggy said. Well, rub-a-dub-dub, what did she have to feel guilty about? She felt dirty, not guilty. She felt stupid, humiliated, used.

Hallie walked back to the living room. She stopped at the corner of the corridor where Roger's picture hung. "Hey, did you hear the one about . . ." she began. She caught herself and stopped. But the ugly joke played itself out in her mind.

It was a Hollywood joke, so ancient that the one-liner was a part of movie mythology. A starlet flounces onto the set, bats her eyelashes, wriggles her hips, and asks loudly: "Who do you have to sleep with to get a part in this picture?"

Bud Broderick had asked that question. Three years ago at a cocktail party in New York, he'd actually asked the hostess who at the party could do the most to further his career. The hostess led him across the room directly to Hallie. "Bud Broderick, Hallie Martin—just the gal you're looking for."

Hallie had blushed. Bud had laughed. The hostess, six months later—while Hallie was recuperating from the affair—had married Bud Broderick, and "How-I-got-Bud-launched-and-Hallie-laid" became her favorite party joke . . . until a friend of Hallie's, a writer with a notoriously fast fist and short fuse, caught the hostess right in the middle of her punch line.

The phone rang again. It was Morgan, next door. "I threw the bum out again," she said.

"I know. I saw the doormat."

"How's Roger?"

Hallie picked up one of the postcards. "He's in Hunan."

"I like Cantonese better."

"What?"

"Hunan's too spicy. Or maybe I'm thinking of Szechuan . . ."

"Morgan, he's not in a Chinese restaurant—he's in China. . . . What are you smoking?"

"What have you got?"

Hallie laughed. Morgan St. James was a star, a dancer who'd done Broadway and ballet and who'd had works created exclusively for her. She was exquisite on stage and endearingly flaky off. She enjoyed surprising people; she adored shocking them. And she was utterly without pretensions. It was her opinion that dancers were the stewardesses of the creative arts.

"I heard you crying," Morgan said.

"Oh, God!" Hallie was stymied. "Morgan, I pay twelve hundred a month for this rooftop paradise. How the hell can you hear through my walls?"

"We-ell . . . I didn't hear you. I mean, I did. But, I saw you first. I was bored. I went for a walk on the terrace. Can I come in?"

"Do I have a choice?"

"Not if you want me to water your plants over the weekend."

Morgan sat on the bed while Hallie packed.

"I don't believe it," she said.

"Well, he did. He got my number and he called and he asked me to be fair . . ."

"I don't believe it."

"Fair?! I'm a reporter! I'm a newsperson! *I'm fair!!*"

"I don't like William Buckley. I mean, I think he looks okay . . . until he starts to speak. Then he looks ab-so-lute-ly *nuts!*"

"What does Buckley have to do with this?"

Morgan shrugged her lovely, broad shoulders. "Well, he's famous, too. And he's a . . . newsperson. And . . . I'm not so sure about the fair part, you know. It all depends where you're coming from."

"Morgan, hand me that skirt, will you?"

Morgan passed the skirt to Hallie. "So what happens after Vegas? You going to be in town for a while?"

"For a little while. Then I'm going to Paris to cover the elections. Roger will probably be in England and meet me later. I miss him."

Morgan tossed her head back dramatically. It was her thoughtful posture. She stared at the beamed ceiling in Hallie's bedroom, then lowered her head and turned her delicate face to the oak chest on which a smaller, more intimate collection of photographs was arranged.

"Roger's perfect. Bud is the pits. Hallie . . . there must be something in between—someone!"

Hallie shut the suitcase. "Aw, I don't know. You kissed one frog, you kissed 'em all. Good night, Morgan."

# 5.

# THE AMPCO TOWER

A maintenance crew wearing mustard-colored coveralls hacked through the underbrush at the base of the Ampco Tower. Browning palmetto leaves and palm fronds, shriveled hibiscus and azalea blossoms, were pruned and tossed into Ampco Running Horse Wheelbarrows. The soil was being enriched with Rising Star-brand Fertilizer and watered through Ampco Champion Underground Sprinkler Systems. The glaring white cement of the plaza in front of the building was being washed down. Not a single dead leaf or cigarette butt or gum wrapper would mar the perfection of the gleaming glass-fronted structure that housed the executive offices of Ampco Industries. In the center of the plaza, a sculptured version of the Ampco running horse was being

polished with Thoroughbred, Ampco's Gentle In-
dustrial-Strength Cleanser.

Hunt Sears stared down at the horse and then
out at a commanding panorama of Los Angeles.
His hands were locked behind his back. His nails
were manicured. He heard papers being shuffled
on the enormous conference table behind him.
That would be Dietrich or Fitzgerald. Toland was
not so easily ruffled by his presence. The chairman
of the board turned slowly. Fitzgerald stopped
toying with the papers and clasped his hands
together like a nervous schoolboy. Sears smiled.

"The rumors are out about Unibank," he announced. He waited for the murmurings around
the table to cease. Then he took his place at the
head of the table.

"By the time the merger is complete, we should
be up twenty dollars a share." He turned to
Dietrich, who was tapping the eraser end of his
sterling pencil on the black marble table. Dietrich
stopped. "Have you placed the announcement?"
Sears asked.

"Full page in the *New York* and *Los Angeles
Times,* and *The Wall Street Journal,* all timed to
hit opening day in Vegas."

"You understand how important Las Vegas is?"

Two heads bobbed in unison—Dietrich's Prus-
sian blond and Fitzgerald's curly dark head. Toland
merely blinked his steel-gray eyes in acknowledg-
ment. He had thinning brown hair, which he
wore slicked down and back like Sears. He wore
wire-rimmed glasses like Sears, as well. But what
passed for a touch of conservatism on the chiseled, tennis-tanned features of the chairman of
the board, looked grave on Toland, and gave him
the air of a perpetually angry accountant.

"Unibank," Sears continued, "is the largest acquisition we've ever attempted. The impression we create at the convention *may* be the deciding factor. I want it all to go perfectly there."

"Ah . . . about the cowboy," Fitzgerald, Ampco's public relations officer, said.

"What about him?" Sears snapped.

Fitzgerald started to shuffle through his papers again as if the answer to Sears' question was hidden among them. "Well, I've got to tell you," he said, scanning a pink sheet that Sears knew contained nothing more than the convention's schedule of events, ". . . he's not behaving well . . . and I wonder if he should be at the convention at all."

"We can't afford to wonder. He either should or shouldn't be at the convention. Which is it?" When Fitzgerald hesitated, Sears turned to Toland. "Is he useful? Can he help us?"

"Ranch Breakfast sales are up," Toland responded crisply. "Research indicates Steele is a factor. If you'd like to see the data . . ."

Sears shook his head. If Toland said something, it was not necessary to confirm it. "Is he integrated into the program?"

Dietrich tapped the folder in front of him with his pencil. One tap this time, authoritative, firm. "Yes, very much so. He'll be at the press conference, of course. And they've worked out something with him and the horse at the show. Then also at the stockholders' reception."

Fitzgerald started to speak. Sears cut him off. "What about Bud Broderick?" he asked.

"He'll be there," Fitzgerald said, "with Joanna."

"Joanna?" Sears stared hard at Fitzgerald.

"Joanna Camden," he amended quickly. Everyone knew that the young actress had given her all to co-star in Ampco's latest epic. And it was rumored that Hunt Sears was the recipient. "Sunday afternoon we're going to preview the film."

"Good."

"What about the cowboy?"

"We'd better go ahead as planned," Sears said, dismissing the subject. "Find a way to handle him."

In his office, two floors below the conference room and three below Hunt Sears' suite, Fitzgerald pondered the problem of Sonny Steele. The first thing to do was to take care of Steele's current commitments. His Ampco baby-sitters had consistently poor reports to offer. Steele was drinking. Steele was late. Steele couldn't remember his lines. Steele kept confusing the two products he was paid to endorse.

Fitzgerald phoned Kevin Ashwood, who was in charge of the regional public relations men, the corps of clean, screened, wholesome go-getters who wore the Ampco crest on their blazers and chaperoned Steele and a host of other celebrities on behalf of the company. "Find a way to handle him," Fitzgerald told Ashwood, "Sears' orders."

Ashwood had an assistant check Sonny Steele's bookings for the day. The cowboy was scheduled to appear at three events: the opening of a fast-food franchise that had agreed to feature Ranch Breakfast on its morning menu in exchange for giveaway glasses with Sonny Steele's smiling likeness on them; a midday TV talk show; and an appearance at a minor-league baseball game. Ashwood looked at his watch. Steele would be on his way to the talk show by now.

"Get hold of our man over there," Kevin Ashwood told Metzger, his assistant. "Tell him that Hunt Sears himself wants to see an improvement in the situation. Tell him to find a way to handle Steele."

Metzger phoned the television station and got the Ampco representative on the line. "Orders from the top, Whitey. Find a way to handle your prima donna . . . or else."

Sonny arrived at the stadium late, as usual. He roared up in his white Cadillac convertible, hurtled over the door, and headed quickly toward the trailer where Leroy and Wendell were waiting to stuff him into another beaded, bangled, sequined, and spangled light-up cowboy suit. His head was down and he was chewing on the tip of his thick, sandy blond mustache when the Ampco man called out to him.

"Ah . . . I had some car trouble," he mumbled, sneaking a glance at his watch. "I'm going to change right now." But, for once, the Ampco man didn't look annoyed. In fact, he looked pleased.

"No rush. Come with me a minute."

Sonny tried to smile, but something, the smug curl of the man's lips, the knot of premonition that had suddenly lodged in his stomach, maybe both, stopped him. Confused, he followed the Ampco representative under the stands to a place where they could see the field. As they reached it, the lights dimmed and the announcer's voice echoed through the stadium's amplifiers:

"Ladies and gentlemen, for Country Breakfast . . . the world's greatest cowboy . . . Mr. Sonny Steele!"

The knot of premonition tightened icily. Suddenly, out of the dark, a rider in a suit of light appeared and began to make a grand circle around the field. The crowd in the stands stomped and cheered.

"That's not . . ." He couldn't continue. Stunned, he stared at the twinkling silhouette on horseback.

"They don't know it," the Ampco man said.

Sonny turned to him, mute, incredulous. The man was smiling. He was beaming with pride and pleasure.

"You can't . . ." Sonny began again. "That ain't . . . honest . . . It . . ." And then he stopped, because he realized that whoever or whatever was riding around the ball park inside that suit of lights was every bit as real and honest a Sonny Steele as he was. His hand went automatically to the knot in the pit of his stomach. It found his silver buckle, instead. He moved his hand away quickly.

## 6.

# LAS VEGAS

Wendell was picking at the underside of his beard. He did that when he was nervous. Picked. Leroy kept glancing down at him, wishing he would stop.

"You going for oil?" he said finally.

Wendell didn't answer. His cool blue eyes settled briefly on the tall, young cowboy, then resumed their vigil.

"You see that cut-out they got of Sonny?"

Wendell nodded.

A waitress in a toga hurried by with a tray of drinks. Leroy took two and offered one to Wendell. The older man blinked at the frosty glass, shook his head, and kept on picking.

Around them, the lobby of Caesar's Palace swarmed with activity. Ampco men in mustard-colored blazers were putting the final touches on their display booths. Promotional films were being tested on closed-circuit TV sets. A huge cut-out of an Ampco earth mover was poised to dig into a papier-mâché hill. A frowning dark-haired man was addressing a platoon of smiling blondes, all wearing Ampco Hospitality Hostess pins. Beyond the girls, beyond the "Welcome" signs and color-coded directional arrows leading everywhere, the vast gambling casino was bustling with action. Ampco men patrolled the aisles, offering free chips to guests wearing Ampco identification tags.

Wendell seemed not to notice the chaos. His eyes stayed fixed on the entrance to the hotel.

"You hear anything?" Leroy asked softly.

With an air of finality, Wendell plucked out one wiry white hair, grimaced, and quit foraging in his peppery beard. "Not a word."

"That's what you get—letting him drive."

"If a man wants to drive his car, let him drive his own damned car. He's not six years old!"

"He's probably drunk in Barstow," Leroy ventured. He took an experimental sip of one of the drinks and spit it back into the glass.

Wendell shook his head. "What'd you expect with a fruit salad floating in it?"

Leroy set down the drinks. "You seen the horse yet? My God, he is something."

"No."

"Want to?"

"No."

"He's just outside, Wendell. In the parking lot. Come on. It'll take your mind off of Sonny."

"What the hell's a thoroughbred racehorse doing in a parking lot in this weather, I'd like to know?"

Leroy shrugged. "They've got him in this corral . . ."

"They got a racehorse in a corral in a parking lot in the middle of Las Vegas in one-hundred-one-degree heat with about a thousand cars driving by every minute . . ."

"Uh-oh, here comes trouble." Leroy raised his big jaw and lowered his hat as Toland approached.

The Ampco executive was polishing his wire-rimmed glasses with a white handkerchief. A running horse was embroidered on one edge of the cloth. "Mr. Hixson," Toland said in a voice bristling with impatience, "where's your client? Danny Miles is waiting to rehearse him."

"Who's Danny Miles?" Leroy asked.

Wendell elbowed the tall boy and smiled weakly at the steely eyed man. "Well, he *just* now called me, Mr. Toland. He's on his way."

There was a commotion at the door. One of the toga-clad hostesses serving complimentary champagne gasped loudly. The group of guests around her turned to the door, straining to see who had come in. Toland put his glasses back on and followed their gaze. Bud Broderick, the star of Ampco General's new film, was trying to make his way through a crowd of jostling fans, press, and photographers. Toland hurried toward him.

"Well, now," Leroy said when the executive was out of earshot, "that was about as close as you'd want to cut it. . . . What do you figure the chances are they got Turkey at the bar?"

Wendell raised an eyebrow at the retreating back of Toland. "Got turkeys all over this place."

"I mean Wild Turkey *bourbon*. Come on, Wendell, let's get us a drink . . . please."

"Sure. What the hell. There's a first time for everything."

"Won't be the first time we ever had a drink together."

"Be the first time we ever had one given to us by some sweet thing wrapped up in a butt-high bedsheet."

"First time for everything," Leroy agreed.

There was another outcry at the entrance as a military man arrived in a limousine decorated with flags. The stars and stripes and the Ampco running horse rode side by side on the hood of the long black Lincoln from which the handsome, white-haired officer debarked. Fitzgerald, in a plaid blazer and dark trousers, made an attempt to slick down his curly hair as he moved through the gaping crowd to welcome the man. Flash bulbs popped as the harried public relations executive and the distinguished-looking general shook hands and smiled for the press.

"Ashwood," Fitzgerald called. He clapped the general on the back and passed him along to Kevin Ashwood, who shook his hand and managed to turn him toward another group of waiting photographers. The general's gracious smiled never faltered. "See you at the press conference, sir. Mr. Ashwood, here, will see that you're all set up. Ashwood, register the general."

Fitzgerald hurried across the lobby to the bank of service elevators where cases of camera equipment stenciled WBC DIGEST were being unloaded. "Hi, there," he said, leading gamely with his throbbing right hand. He couldn't remember how many hands he'd shaken since daybreak, but his own seemed to be keeping a painful tally. "I'm Joe Fitzgerald, Ampco's public relations officer. Anything I can do, you just let me know."

"Bernie Stieg, 'WBC Digest' . . ."

"Where's the hospitality suite?" a mustachioed young man, wearing a WBC crew cap, asked.

". . . and this is Chris, our sound man."

Fitzgerald pumped Chris' hand. "Welcome aboard. Hospitality suite's just around that corner, but you boys can just mug any of our hostesses down here and get yourselves a champagne on Ampco. Miss Martin arrive okay?"

"Over there," Bernie said and turned back to supervise the unloading of his equipment.

"'Mug'?" Chris shook his head when Fitzgerald had left.

"Don't let it bother you. It's just how L.A. types relate to New York."

Hallie was staring up at the twice-life-size cutout of Sonny Steele in his light-up cowboy suit when Fitzgerald found her.

"Hi, there, Hallie. All checked in yet?"

"Fitz. Hello. Boyd's taking care of it, thanks."

"Buy you a drink?"

Templeton joined them. "Seducing the working press already, Fitz?" He shook Fitzgerald's hand. "It won't work on Hallie. You ought to know that by now. Only shot you've got is to give up a story."

Fitzgerald smiled professionally. "Look around," he said. "There's a hell of a story here—fashion, food, films . . ."

Hallie took off the wide-brimmed felt hat she was wearing and shook her newly cut hair loose. It fell into perfect layers waving softly back from her handsome cheekbones.

"Nice," Fitzgerald said. "How do you stay so trim and chic?"

Chris, the WBC sound man, was passing by. "She eats a balanced diet, gets plenty of rest, and mugs designers on Seventh Avenue each season. . . . My anchorwoman." He sighed. "I think I'll keep her."

"Thanks," Hallie said. "Where's Bernie?"

"On his way. He's just making sure the camera gear's safe. See you."

"What time's the press conference?" Hallie asked Fitzgerald.

"Relax, Hallie. You've got hours yet. Have you seen your room? You're going to love it. A real lady's room—all pretty and pink . . ."

Bernie joined them. "Did I hear right? They got you booked into the Ladies' Room, Hallie?"

"Just until she learns to relax," Boyd said.

"Are you kidding? Look at her. If she were any more relaxed, she'd be asleep."

Hallie was smiling. At least, her lips, which tended normally to purse, were turned up slightly at the corners. It was the best she could do. Her green eyes were glazed with boredom as she surveyed the crowded lobby. Boyd Templeton took her arm and led her toward the elevators. Fitzgerald walked along with them.

Flash bulbs flashed as new celebrities arrived. Everyone seemed to know everyone else. There was a great deal of loud laughter and hand-shaking and back-slapping going on. In the general chaos, a very pretty blonde woman in her early thirties approached the front desk. She was alone and looked a bit intimidated by the confusion from which she'd just emerged. She wasn't wearing an Ampco tag, Hallie noticed. And she was very voluptuous.

The woman leaned toward the desk clerk. She had to raise her voice above normal to make herself heard. Hallie picked up the Southern twang immediately, but not the words. A call girl was her first guess. But the woman seemed too tentative, too shy. Hallie chided herself for the bigotry that made her automatically ascribe the combination of traits—a seductive Southern accent, platinum-blonde hair, and a voluptuous figure—to a hooker. In fact, the woman looked familiar.

"Who's that, Fitz?"

Fitzgerald looked over at the blonde and shrugged. "No idea. Won't take me a minute to find out, though. . . ."

The elevator arrived. "No. Thanks, anyway," Hallie said.

Fitzgerald waved to the merry band of salesmen and stockholders who exited. Then he held the door back for the WBC crew and stepped inside with them.

"What time is the press conference?" Bernie asked Hallie.

She shrugged and leaned her head back against a corner of the mirrored car and listened distractedly to Templeton and Fitzgerald. She couldn't remember where she'd seen the blonde woman before. And she was bored. The rituals of sales conferences and conventions were tediously repetitious: the enthusiastic greetings, the free-flowing booze, and forced gaiety of the good old boys; the "no holds barred" press conference, where every question was anticipated and every answer rehearsed; the plastic-covered name tags that said "Hello! My name is . . ." in case you were too anti-social to say hello yourself or too sloshed to remember what your name was. . . .

"*Story*, Fitz—what can you give us in the way of story?" Templeton was pressing Fitzgerald.

The P.R. man ran his hand through his curly

hair, then patted it into place as he answered. "Well, we have half-a-dozen movie stars. You just saw Bud Broderick come in. . . ."

Had she? Hot damn. She'd heard the squealing and screaming, but she *hadn't* seen Bud Broderick come in. She'd seen a glossy head of hair professionally grayed at the temples; a tan the sun would disavow but which Ampco Bronzing Gel might take credit for; dark glasses and white teeth —and all that was missing from both were the price tags.

"Rising Star's here," Fitzgerald continued. He sounded very down-home; about six-figures-a-year smooth, Hallie thought. "And we got the biggest damned Earth Mover you ever saw—"

"What're you doing with the horse?" Templeton asked.

"We've worked out a little presentation with Sonny Steele—you know, the cowboy we use for Country Breakfast."

Bernie turned to Hallie. "Worth covering?"

"Well," Fitzgerald cut in nervously, "there's better stuff. The cowboy's a peach of a guy, but not terrific copy. Lots of 'yup' and 'shucks'. . . . He's no interview. I'd steer clear."

Hallie's eyes opened slightly. The flicker of interest went unnoticed. Steele—The Electric Horseman, she remembered. Then, disconcertingly, the image of the blonde woman in the lobby came to mind. The blonde and Sonny Steele . . . Hallie tried to make the connection. She'd seen the woman in one of the pieces of film Anne had screened for her in New York. Maybe. In the early rodeo sequences? The woman had shorter hair then, curled in one of those awful little-girl styles . . . a "flip" or something. She was the one to whom Steele had tossed one of his silver championship buckles. Maybe.

The woman downstairs was older, but then, of course, she would be. Older, blonder, her hair was long and straight now; her body was fuller, voluptuous, more mature. Was she Steele's wife? Girl friend? A rodeo groupie? Was there such a thing? Hallie wondered suddenly. Were there girls who "serviced" rodeo heros the way there were girls who slept with rock stars or football heros, or, for that matter, television "personalities" . . . ?

The thought made her uncomfortable. Was that a little too close to home, Hallie, old girl? she chided herself. Are you still worried about who wants what from you, and why?

"Concentrate on other things," Fitzgerald was saying.

Amen, Hallie thought.

The elevator doors opened. "This way, please." The bellman stepped out into the corridor and waited for Hallie, Boyd, and Bernie to follow.

"See you downstairs," Fitzgerald called as the doors closed.

"Yup . . ." Hallie said. "So they don't want us to interview the cowboy."

Bernie glanced at the numbers and arrows on the wall opposite the elevator. "I'm down this way. Listen, where do you want to start? I've got to get a sandwich."

"What do you mean, where do I want to start?" Boyd was following the bellman. Hallie smiled at Bernie. "With the cowboy, of course."

"Right. Catch you later."

She hurried to catch up with Boyd. They followed the bellman down the long, carpeted corridor. "Why're they so uptight about talking to Steele?" Hallie asked after a moment.

"Beats me. . . . Anybody in particular you want to interview?"

"I've got some thoughts," she said.

"You're right here, Miss Martin." The bellman unlocked the door.

"Boyd, is the cowboy on tap for the press conference?"

"Check your list," he said.

"Which one—the blue list or the pink or the green . . . ?"

"Call room service and ask them to have an investigative journalist sent up."

She pulled off her earrings and went inside. The room wasn't bad at all. It wasn't the cherry-vanilla confection she'd expected from Fitzgerald's description. It was large with windows that over-looked the distant mountains. The bed was sepa-rated from the sitting area by a carpeted platform. The headboard was fan-shaped and reminded her of a Thirties movie set. She wished she'd packed her slinky pink nightgown. It was just the sort of Harlowesque costume in which to lounge on a bed with a fan-shaped headboard that rested on a plushly carpeted platform.

She tossed her attaché case into a chair and fell back onto the bed. It was pretty firm for a hotel bed. Lord knew, she'd had her fill of sway-back monsters that pinched your butt like the spirit of Shriners past. She rolled over and off the bed.

On a desk near the window, a pretty bouquet of flowers sat in a little vase. There was a card propped between the baby's breath and one of the pink tea roses. Hallie picked up the little envelope.

Bud or Roger? she wondered. She took out the card. It was from Morgan St. James. She read it and laughed.

"You wouldn't even smear your lip gloss if you did it right . . . ! Love, Morgan."

Beside the vase was the Ampco convention itinerary for opening day. Beneath the schedule of events was a folder on which the corporate logo was embossed. She opened the folder. Inside was a sheaf of press releases and another identification badge; this one had the word PRESS printed on it. She picked it up. Thanks for the reminder, she thought, bouncing the plastic-covered badge in her palm. The only way out is to *work* it out. She smiled and tossed the badge back onto the desk. To work, to work. She rubbed her hands together, fished a cigarette from her purse, and stuck it, unlit, between her teeth. Then she dialed the front desk.

"Sonny Steele's room, please." She chewed on the filter tip as she waited for the cowboy to answer. If he wasn't in his room, she might have him paged. Probably not. After Fitzgerald's cautiously couched warning, she'd do better to sniff around quietly for a while. She glanced over the itinerary. Steele was scheduled to appear at the press conference. Perhaps she'd have to wait until then.

She was about to hang up when someone answered. "Hello? That you? Where you been?"

"Hello," Hallie said. "Is Mr. Steele there, please?"

"Ah . . . who is this?"

"My name is Hallie Martin. I was wondering if . . ."

"You with Ampco?"

"No. I'd like to . . ."

"Shoot! Don't you gals never give up? Now, Sonny ain't here, and far as you're concerned, he ain't going to be, if you get my meaning. He's got some serious business to take care of here, and we'd sure appreciate it if ya'll let up on the boy awhile."

"Who is this?" Hallie asked. She had some inkling of who "ya'll" might be. She reached for the attaché case, where her clipboard and pad were packed. Yes, Virginia, there are rodeo groupies, she thought. And the man on the other end of this phone thinks I'm one.

"This is Mr. Sonny Steele's manager."

"Oh. Well, hello. I think there may be a misunderstanding here. I'm with 'WBC Digest'—the television news magazine . . ." She could practically hear the man sucking air. "My name is Hallie Martin." She waited for it to sink in.

"Well, I'm real sorry, ma'am," he said after a moment. "My name is Wendell Hixson. Like I said, ma'am, I'm Sonny's manager, and, well, he gets all kinda calls, you know."

"Of course," Hallie said. She pulled the pad out and scrawled the name Wendell Hixson on it. "Is Mr. Steele in, please?"

"No, ma'am, he ain't."

"Oh. I see. Ah . . . Mr. Hixson, do you think we might chat for a while? Informally, of course. Over a drink. I'll meet you in the bar downstairs—" She looked at the hotel directory that was under the glass on the desk. "Cleopatra's Barge, it's called. . . . In fifteen minutes?"

"Well, I tell you, ma'am . . ."

"Make that twenty, Mr. Hixson. How will I recognize you?"

"Call me Wendell. You won't have no trouble. I'll probably recognize you."

She showered and changed. According to the itinerary, the press conference would begin in an hour. Best foot forward, she told herself as she stood before the full-length mirror. She was wearing long high-heeled, butter-soft boots that peek-a-booed out of the thigh-high slit in her skirt. A fair amount of flesh flashed between the top of the boots and the side seam of the skirt, but the blouse she'd chosen was high-necked and demure. The outfit would see her through the press conference and, depending on how long that ran, the cocktail party later. She brushed her hair quickly, grabbed a pair of chunky earrings, checked the tape in her miniature recorder, and hurried out to meet Steele's manager.

He was sitting at a small round table in the bar. He had a full beard that he was raking with his fingers. The hair on his head, what she could see of it beneath the broad brim of his cowboy hat, was gray, long, and tied back in a ponytail. In contrast, the hair on his face was a faded straw-berry-blond color threaded through with coarse white hairs. He stood as she entered the bar area and waited until she'd settled into her seat before he took his again. He was rough-hewn but had a sweet, courtly air about him, and his blue eyes took in every line of her costume and most of the curves beneath it.

"Well, I'm real glad to meet you," he said. "Why, you're about ten times prettier than your pictures."

They ordered drinks. Hallie put the tape recorder on the table.

"Where is Mr. Steele?" she asked. She hadn't

started the machine yet, but Hixson was staring at it uncomfortably.

"Oh, he's driving in. He'll be along any time now."

"I guess I'll see him at the press conference, then."

"Yes ma'am." He glanced past her, beyond the bar area that overlooked the casino, toward the hotel entrance.

A bosomy waitress brought their drinks. She was wearing a toga and her hair was pinned up. It sat like a cruller on the top of her head. Except for the costume and a set of false eyelashes so thick and heavy that her lids were at half-mast, she looked like any bone-weary, middle-aged waitress. When she left, Hallie pressed the "Start" button on the recorder and Wendell sighed softly.

"That's a very unusual watchband," she said. She checked the volume needle as she spoke. It hovered in the right range to pick up a conversational tone.

"Thank you, ma'am. It's Indian." He sipped his bourbon, smiled politely, and looked past her toward the door.

"May I see it?"

Wendell took off his watch and handed it to her. It was silver and turquoise and heavier than it looked. Hallie slipped it on her own slender wrist. "It's lovely." She handed the watch back to him. "Listen," she continued casually, "why would Ampco ask us not to interview Sonny Steele?"

"Where'd you hear that?"

"One of your Ampco people."

Wendell reached under his beard and began to stroke his neck. "Well . . . that don't mean anything. They're just a little down on Sonny right now. . . . He ain't been acting himself lately. He's a cowboy . . . sometimes he loses the best part of himself."

"What's the best part of himself?"

"Oh, you'd have to know him a long time to know that."

Hallie smiled. Evasive as the response sounded, she believed it. She believed him. He didn't like the tape recorder. He didn't like the idea of being interviewed, however informally. He didn't appear to think much of the convention or of the people who were running it and were "a little down on Sonny right now." But his eyes, when they looked at her instead of at the door, were very direct. Nothing personal, they seemed to say. You've got your job; I've got mine.

"How long have *you* known him?" she asked.

"Oh, a long, long time. Before his daddy died. He came up to my knee . . ."

Hallie glanced over at his watch. There was time. Sooner or later, if the blonde was someone important to Sonny Steele, Wendell would get around to it.

# 7.

# CIRCUS MAXIMUS

The sun was a bloody yolk melting into the mountaintops. Beneath it, the million lights of Las Vegas leaped out at him—from billboards, gambling palaces, motels, hotels, and architectural wonders beyond classification. Sonny had worn his dark glasses against the desert's glare. He kept them on though it was dusk, because sunlight was benevolent compared to the garish circus through which he now rode.

All the blinding, blinking lights flashed a welcome to one of their own. They winked as if he were family. Never mind that he was flesh and they were not. They shared a mission beyond such distinctions. They were—Sonny Steele and all the lights of Las Vegas—created equal . . . to amaze and amuse, to razzle-dazzle the rubes, to blaze and bring in the bucks. All the blinking, blinding lights vied for his attention, but the ones that lit the hitchhiking cowboy mounted to the front of a block-long casino won out. Sonny slowed down just to stare at the smiling, illuminated giant whose mechanical arm beckoned to every passing stranger. Then he gunned the motor of his dusty white Cadillac and headed down the strip.

He'd driven hard. Both he and the car looked it as he pulled into the parking lot of Caesar's Palace and wove between the rows of Mercedes and Rollses. He parked haphazardly, then hurried from the car toward the hotel. He was almost at the curved entrance when he noticed the luxurious horse van parked a few yards away. Then he saw Rising Star's corral. He stopped abruptly and made his way through the crowd that stood gaping at the magnificent stallion.

The corral turned out to be made of plastic. Heavy white plastic logs surrounded a piece of blue AstroTurf spread out on the steaming, oil-stained pavement of the parking lot. Sonny took off his sunglasses. Through red-rimmed eyes, he studied the horse until Wendell's voice shouted out for him. "Sonny!! Sonny, damn it, where've you been?!"

Wendell rushed up, grabbed his arm, and dragged him toward the entranceway. "Jesus, boy, what happened to you? Come on, now! Where in blazes you been all this while?!"

He turned back to catch a last glimpse of the big bay. "What the hell's that horse doing in the middle of a parking lot?"

"I don't know," Wendell said, "but he got here on time! Come on!!"

There weren't too many photographers left

hanging around the front of the hotel. Sonny didn't bother to smile for the ones there were. Flash bulbs popped. People turned to stare. A couple in Western-style clothing called his name and waved. Someone asked if he were a movie star. "I know that face," a man said.

Wendell hurried him through the lobby. "The press conference has already started. . . . Danny Miles has been waiting all day to rehearse you. . . ."

Sonny grabbed a drink off the tray of a passing waitress. "What've they got me doing now? Sitting on that flagpole out front?"

"Son, there's been hell to pay around here . . . all them news people—so behave, will you? Just behave."

"Who the hell's Danny Miles?" he asked, polishing off the drink. Wendell took the glass from his hand.

Leroy hurried over. "Blow in my face," he said, walking along fast with them. "You smell like a tequila factory. Here. Take a couple of these."

"No more of them pills," Wendell snapped.

"They're Tic-Tacs."

"You won't guess who I seen," Sonny said. He took a handful of the little breath mints from Leroy and popped them into his mouth. "Rush and Hawkman and old Edgar Stone—they all send 'hello.' And Foggy Tates' wife, Louise—she gave me this handkerchief." He pulled a silk hanky from his pocket and sniffed it lavishly.

"I told you he was in Barstow," Leroy said.

"Smells just like her. . . . Damn, they got pretty girls in Las Vegas!"

"Come on, now. Sonny. They're real serious about this stuff, these people. I never seen them so nervous. They are really uptight. Company's trying to buy up a big bank and they don't want nothing to go wrong. They want everything to go just perfect."

They reached the door to the conference room. "What's in here?"

"Press conference! And you're late. Now, don't tell no jokes and don't lift up nobody's skirts."

"What do I have to do?"

"Nothing . . . if we're lucky."

Sonny stopped suddenly and turned to Wendell. His bloodshot gaze fastened pleadingly on the bearded cowboy's resolute eyes. "Aw, Wendell . . . Wendell, please . . ."

Wendell opened the door and pushed him into the room. The conference was in progress. Not many of the reporters turned to look at him. They were seated on folding chairs behind long, cloth-covered tables, facing the dais. Fitzgerald saw him, though. And Dietrich. The blond executive was sneering. He was always sneering. The features of his face fell naturally into an expression of annoyance, and not even the smile he wore now for the press made a significant change in that. It was an unfortunate lopsided little smile that could just as easily pass for a sneer.

Dietrich sat at the far end of the table on the dais. He was conducting the press conference—almost literally. He used his silver lead pencil like a baton. He tapped the table with it and acknowledged reporters by pointing the gleaming pencil at them. As Sonny hurried up the side aisle to take his place beside an august general, Dietrich's eyes assessed him meanly.

"But isn't it true that Unibank violently opposes a takeover?" a reporter asked. "That their board of directors has promised an all-out war against you?"

"Just a moment," Dietrich interrupted. "This isn't a takeover. This is a merger."

"But . . . Omnibank has always fought take-overs . . . mergers, isn't that true?"

"We think that attitude is changing. We have made a generous offer for the Omnibank shares, and we are confident they will accept. . . ."

Sonny slouched in his chair. He was tired and thirsty, but the water pitcher was down at Die-trich's end of the table. It was actually between Dietrich and the movie star. To get at it, he'd have had to reach across the general and the pretty girl sitting to the right of Bud Broderick. He put his hands on the table and, unconsciously, began to drum on it. He was hitting the table very softly. There was no real noise to speak of, but the general turned and shot him a look, and Sonny repented, smiling and folding his hands.

One of the reporters in the audience had seen the exchange. A woman. A very good-looking woman with pale brown, shining hair and green eyes and slender shoulders that curved forward slightly, but not enough to hide the impressive, unharnessed breasts that nuzzled against the flowing fabric of her blouse. She saw him staring at her, too, and didn't flinch.

"I don't know where you get *your* information," Dietrich said, "but in my opinion, the Unibank board is made up of serious, intelligent business-men. . . ." He pointed his pencil at another re-porter. "Troy Reed looks about ready to jump out of his skin. What's your question, Troy?"

"Bud"—the balding, chunky man Dietrich had called upon stood up—"you've played opposite just about every major actress. Who, in your opinion, is the best . . ."—he hesitated playfully— ". . . ah . . . kisser?"

Most of the reporters chuckled. The woman with the green eyes did not. Her expression as she studied Sonny was deadpan, serious. There was the smallest suggestion of curiosity in it, as if she wondered what he was doing there; what someone *like* him was doing sitting beside a general, an actress, and a genuine movie star.

"That would depend on what part of the body you have in mind," Broderick replied to the reporter's question. The answer got a big laugh.

Sonny glanced at Broderick and shook his head. The gesture was barely perceptible. But somehow he had the feeling that the lady with the curious green eyes and sweet breasts had probably caught it.

"And I dare you to print *that!*" Bud Broderick yelled over the laughter.

Suddenly, the green-eyed lady was on her feet.

"Mr. Steele, why'd you come forty-five minutes late for the press conference?" she demanded.

The question quieted the room. Everybody seemed vaguely discomforted by its directness, especially Fitzgerald, who had been sitting near her and who now lowered his head and covered his face with his hands. The woman, however, stood up straight and serious, waiting for a reply. Sonny noticed that the clipboard she was holding was pressed against the front of her blouse. He smiled. He guessed it was a mean smile.

"I was getting my nails done," he said. It got a laugh. "Got another one?"

"I'm thinking," she told him.

"Well, hurry it up. These people got important

business . . . and I just found out the bar's only open twenty-four hours."

Fitzgerald checked the response around the room before he decided that the remark merited a smile.

Hallie pointed to the running horse logo which was on the wall behind the dais. "Pound for pound," she said, "who's worth more . . . you or the horse?"

The room was quiet again. Reporters and executives were caught up in the odd interchange. Sonny stopped smiling. He stared at her silently for a second. Then he said softly, "I don't want to tangle with you, lady."

Dietrich stood quickly. "Mr. Steele's idea is a good one. The bar is open. Let's adjourn here, and I hope to see you all upstairs at the reception before the show."

The group began to disperse. Sonny stood up slowly. He was still watching Hallie when Wendell rushed up to him. "I told you not to do that. Didn't I say to behave? Come on." He started to usher Sonny from the room.

"I need a drink."

Wendell shook his head. "You've got no *time* for a drink. You got a rehearsal to do. This Danny Miles feller's been waiting on you the whole damned day!!"

The room in which the rehearsal was taking place was a cavernous nightclub called the Circus Maximus. Danny Miles, the famous industrial show director, was wearing a woolen cardigan against the room's excessive air conditioning and gesticulating with his horn-rimmed glasses, when he wasn't chewing on the earpiece of them.

Sonny waited on stage while Miles walked eight bored showgirls through their number.

"Then, you're over there. . . . Lights up . . . form the 'V' . . . turn, kick, and open ranks for the cowboy. You . . ." He beckoned with his glasses to Sonny. "Okay. After the circle, you dismount. Come down to your mark, stage right—"

"Where's the horse?" Sonny asked.

Miles shouted into the wings. "Bring in the damned horse!"

There was a ramp leading from the center of the stage out into the darkened room. A man in yellow pants and a sweater like Miles' hurried from the wings to the head of the ramp. "The horse!" He hollered into the darkness. "Bring him in! Get the horse over here!"

A wrangler led Rising Star up the ramp and maneuvered him to a painted mark on stage.

"Spot, please!" Danny Miles called.

A spotlight sliced through the darkness. The horse gleamed in its glare. "God," Danny Miles said, "he's a beauty. Look at him shine."

Sonny was less enthusiastic. He looked the stallion over appraisingly. He ran his hand down the animal's shoulder, then he smelled his hand. "You'd shine, too," he told the director, "if you were covered with fly spray." His voice sounded as weary as his eyes looked, but there was an edge of anger perceptible in both.

Miles turned to the wrangler who'd led the horse on stage. "Now, Sonny rides in, circles three times—applause, applause, applause—then he dismounts on this mark. Got that? Okay. Now, Sonny . . ."

Sonny wasn't listening. He walked around

Rising Star, patting him, clucking soothingly at him. He heard the horse's labored breathing. "He's got shipping fever," he told the wrangler.

"Sonny, your first line is . . ."

"We had the vet this afternoon," the man said. He spoke slowly, almost apologetically. He was appraising Sonny's handling of the horse. He was not ready to concede him all-out admiration yet, but obviously the famous cowboy could spot shipping fever when he saw it.

"What have you got him on?" Sonny asked impatiently.

"Penicillin," the wrangler said.

Sonny shot him a cynical look.

". . . and a little Bute," the man added softly.

"For that tendon?" Sonny was kneeling, stroking Rising Star's leg very gently. It was hot to the touch and felt swollen. Butazoladine would only dull the pain. And without the pain to inform the animal, to slow him down, the tendon would get worse.

The wrangler nodded in confirmation.

"Should be bandaged," Sonny said. The anger was taking over rapidly.

"They think it don't look right . . . you know, for the public."

He straightened up and stared at the man. "Muscled up pretty good, isn't he . . . ?"

Danny Miles cleared his throat conspicuously. "All right, now. Sonny, the first thing you do after you dismount is you say . . ."

"Your horse is stoned," Sonny told the wrangler.

The man turned his head as if Sonny's glare were painful. He looked off into the wings, then down at his own boots. "How are we going to get him up in front of all these people . . . with lights . . . and these damned cables, and . . ."

"Excuse me, gentlemen!" Miles tapped the palm of his hand with his glasses. "Sonny, your first line is—" He sighed dramatically, then looked at the script his assistant held up for him. "Right. Your first line: you say, 'Ranch Breakfast—a champ's way to start the morning.' Then you look at the horse and you say, 'Ain't that right, Rising Star? If you agree, don't say anything.' That's where the laugh comes." At the director's signal, the assistant handed Sonny the script. "You try it," Miles urged.

The wrangler backed out of the way. Frustrated, Sonny glanced at the horse's leg again, then looked over the script. He began to read aloud in a distracted way. "'Ranch Breakfast—a champ's way to start the morning . . .'" Then he let the script drop to the stage and started away. "Okay, I got that."

"There's more!" Miles shouted after him.

"Yeah. I saw it." He walked out of the spotlight and into the wings.

Miles turned to his assistant, who shrugged. Then he turned to the wrangler. "That's the most discourteous thing I ever saw in the theater!" he told the man. The wrangler looked down at his boots again.

Wendell caught up with Sonny as he left the nightclub. "Where're you going now?"

"Where's that party they're having?" Sonny asked without slowing down. He was headed for the elevators at a good clip. Wendell hurried along behind him.

"You ain't dressed for no party. What happened

in there? Sonny, I can see you're riled about something! Talk to me, boy . . . !"

He was knocking the road dust off his jeans and running his fingers through his sun-bleached hair. He didn't stop. "I got to talk to Mr. Sears. Right now. You going to tell me where that damned party's at?"

"You crazy?!"

At the elevators there was a painted placard sitting on an easel. WELCOME AMPCO! it read. In smaller script beneath the greeting were the words "Hospitality Suite." An arrow pointed to the left of the elevator bank. Sonny walked off in the direction of the arrow.

"Sonny, you got smoke coming out of your ears, boy." Wendell hurried after him. "Why don't we talk first? Just you and me. Have a drink together . . ."

He turned the corner and followed the sounds of music and laughter down the corridor. Wendell tried to keep up. "You're in no shape to talk to no Hunt Sears!"

"What've I got to do first, calisthenics?"

The door to the Hospitality Suite was open. Sonny went in before Wendell could stop him. The place was wall-to-wall people—executives in suits, flunkies in Ampco blazers, salesmen, stockholders, journalists, wives, mistresses, celebrities, misplaced tourists, and a lousy band. He wove his way through the crowd, picking up a drink en route. He tapped the back of a blazer. "Sears here?" he called above the strains of "Fascination" being squeezed out of a glittering red and yellow accordion.

The Ampco man cupped his ear. "Scissors?"

"Your boss!" Sonny shouted.

"Sorry . . . I think he is."

He slugged down the drink and started through the crush again—shaking hands, exchanging greetings, downing drinks, and smiling as he searched for Sears.

"Sonny Steele. I'll be darned. Howdy, partner!" A man in a suit grabbed his hand and started pumping it vigorously. "T. Howard Elkins!" he hollered, pointing at the Ampco name tag on his breast pocket. "Ohio. Just north of Hamilton. You know where Hamilton is?"

"Sure," Sonny said. "Great town. Nice to meet you."

"Listen here, partner. You're just the man I need. I'm buying my boy a horse next month. For his birthday, you know. Well, sir, it'll be his first horse. Me, I didn't even get a bicycle till I was in my teens and worked for it. What kind you think is best for him?"

Sonny pried the man's fingers open and retrieved his hand. "How old's your kid?" he asked, moving off.

The man followed. "Six."

"Then you want a short horse," he said sagely. He gulped another drink and looked around. The lady reporter was across the room. A tall man in a three-piece suit had her cornered. The smile on her face was about as genuine as his own. Her eyes kept moving, looking for a way out. She spotted him, recognized him. Her eyes held his with an awkward intensity. He raised his glass at her and watched as she slipped away from the tall man and started to work her way through the crowd toward him.

"Sonny, there's somebody I'd like you to meet." An Ampco man was tugging at his shirt sleeve.

He brushed the man's hand off and kept his eye on the lady reporter. "Grace Phillips," the Ampco man said. He was as obstinate as a horse fly. This time, he grabbed Sonny's elbow and tried to pull him around to face the woman. Sonny turned sharply, but the man stepped back in time and his elbow only grazed the mustard-colored blazer.

"Mrs. George Phillips," the man said pointedly.

The significance of the name was lost on Sonny. He looked past the middle-aged woman to Hallie. ". . . the mean-question lady," he said.

"Just curious," she called back to him.

"*George Phillips*—the Million-Dollar Club," the Ampco man was practically shouting now. "He sold a million dollars' worth of Ranch Breakfast —*wholesale . . .*"

"You know what curiosity done to the cat," said Sonny.

". . . and this is *Mrs*. Phillips," the man shrilled, "and I want you to meet her!!"

Sonny glanced at the woman and then at the annoying little man who'd taken to pulling at him again. He raised his arms up out of reach, trying not to spill the drink in his hand. "Yeah, you do that," he said, grinning his box-top grin. Then he headed away back into the thick of it. The last glimpse he had of the lady reporter, she was cornered again. And this time the man came up to her chin.

"We met in New York," Sonny heard him say.

"Did we like each other?"

"I don't think so."

Sonny drank to that. He craned over the heads nearby but still didn't see Sears. There was a lavish buffet set up in a corner of the room. He tried to move past it carefully. There were people pressing in on him and he had to maneuver sideways to avoid scraping against the table. He wound up with deviled egg on his belt, anyway. He stopped to get another drink and wipe off the yellow smear. Before he'd finished cleaning up, another Ampco man accosted him.

"It's good to see you, pal. . . . We were a little worried, there. . . ." The man glanced curiously at the mess on his buckle.

Sonny swabbed at it with a cocktail napkin. "Car trouble, Ed."

"Steve."

He tossed the napkin over the man's shoulder onto a table behind him. "Car trouble either way."

"Sure. . . . I want to talk to you about a few things. Salt Lake and that TV show in Denver. We made a little change in your copy. No big thing . . ."

"You seen Sears?"

"Ah . . . does he usually approve copy for you? I . . . no one told me anything about that . . ."

Sonny walked away.

Leroy and Wendell were at the door, which was as far as they could get without fighting the crowd. Leroy, who was almost a head taller than the distraught manager, peered in, searching for Sonny. He shook his head. He had thick black hair, straight and glossy as an Indian's. He had a large nose that he wrinkled in dismay now. "Why'd you leave him go in here in the first place?"

Wendell didn't bother looking at the boy. He thrust his arms forward and separated two bodies that were pressed butt to butt blocking the entrance. Then he burrowed in between them. "For

Chrissakes," he shouted at Leroy, who followed him, "just shut up and find him."

Sonny leaned on the mirrored bar savoring a moment of unexpected privacy. He exhaled slowly and put down his glass. His eyes were still burning from road grit and his head had started thumping again. He rubbed his temples. The veins on his forehead were standing out. They were hard as rope and knotted with tension. He could feel the anger pulsing through them.

He breathed in deeply and exhaled again. It didn't help. He kept thinking about the horse: Rising Star, a thoroughbred stallion, caged up in a stinking parking lot, in a phony corral under the brutal Las Vegas sun. The horse was injured and they were doping him up. The horse was a champion and they were going to hang lights all over him and teach him to dance.

There was a commotion at the door that moved farther into the room. At the center of the excited little knot of people, Sonny saw Bud Broderick.

"Hey, Steele!" the tall actor shouted. "Have you seen my picture?"

He nodded and smiled and turned his back on the star. It didn't work. Broderick and his coterie kept on coming.

"I patterned my whole character after you," Broderick said. He was signing autographs as he spoke. "I did a lot of my own stunts." He looked across the room, smiled, and shouted, "Hi, darling!"

Sonny followed his gaze. It was the lady reporter again. She nodded at Broderick, quickly, coldly.

"Brr," Broderick said, still smiling at her. "Hell hath no fury . . ." He laughed.

"Oh, boy, this is a crazy business we're in, isn't it? Gets to you. I'm looking for a place to get away from it all. You're a cowboy; you know what I mean—someplace where I can just clean up the old brain. Ride out there and breath in the air. Listen." He stuck one of the photographs he'd been signing into Sonny's hands. "I've got to go talk to that broad, for a second. Take care of this for me, will you?" He started through the crowd toward Hallie.

"You know," he called over his shoulder, "when you ride, it looks so real!"

"It is real," Sonny said.

"No! Really?"

Hallie took a step backward. There was nowhere to go. A sea of people at her back and Bud Broderick's capped teeth cruising toward her. Jaws-time, and where the hell was Roy Scheider when you needed him?

"Hello, Hallie." The deep, soft voice. "You're looking . . . swell, Hallie."

"I think that's 'Dolly,' isn't it? 'Hello, *Dolly* . . .' "

"Thanks for the press conference. It means a lot to me. You know, JoAnne and I are separated. She's breaking my balls, Hallie. The woman's gone nuts, I swear. Half of everything's not good enough for her. She wants it all . . . preferably in blood. I don't work, she'll haul my ass into court again. You know, you could have hurt me back there in that conference room . . . but you didn't, and I'm grateful, Hallie. I am deeply grateful."

"You're welcome. Good-bye."

He put his arm around her waist suddenly. A flash bulb popped. He released her. "Thanks.

Nice seeing you, too," he said to the Ampco photographer. "Hey, I hear you're seeing a political heavyweight these days. Senatorial candidate or something? Serious?"

"Very."

He looked wounded. "No! Really?"

"Mr. Broderick . . ." A matron with high and wide lacquered hair pressed a publicity still into his hand. "For Tammy . . . she's my daughter."

"Your *daughter*?" You could have knocked Broderick over with an Oscar. "Honey, your daughter can't be old enough to read yet." He scrawled his signature hastily on a corner of the photo. "Do you know Hallie Martin?" he asked the misty-eyed woman. " 'WBC Digest.' Ever catch it?"

Hallie smiled sweetly. "Don't worry. We're working on a vaccine."

"Oh, I saw you on that show, Mr. Broderick. It was the first time I ever saw you on TV. I remember it very well. In fact, it was the first time I ever saw you anywhere. It was wonderful. I see all your pictures now."

"Well, you just keep on watching Hallie Martin's show because we're going to do it again, right, Hallie?"

"Over your dead body, Bud."

The lady laughed giddily. Broderick took Hallie's arm and dragged her away.

"Let go, Bud. No more free publicity today. You've got all the pictures of us together you're getting at this bash."

"I'm not looking for pictures, Hal. I want the real thing—the *whole* thing."

She ground her spiked New York heel into his L.A. canvas casuals. "Not even if you brought your stunt man with you, buster!" she said, and walked away.

It was over! The evolutionary end of an affair —prince to frog! She wished Roger were here, or Morgan. Sonny Steele was still at the bar. If she could fight through to him, she'd celebrate with a glass of champagne.

Sonny scanned the party again. This time he saw Sears. The chairman of the board was shielded by a group of Ampco executives, one of whom caught the look in Sonny's eye and tried to intercept him before he reached Hunt Sears. But Sears had seen the cowboy coming. "What do you think of our horse?" he asked pleasantly, interrupting the man in Sonny's way. "Couldn't find you a better straight man, could we?"

"No, Mr. Sears, I—"

"You've all met Mr. Steele?" he asked the group. They had. "It's a beautiful animal, isn't it, Sonny?"

"He's an amazing animal . . . except he's not being taken care of." The men were staring at him. They were all smiling, even the one who'd tried to stop him. Their smiles were as thin and uniform as Ampco blazers.

Sears was smiling, too. "I guarantee you that animal gets better care than you and I."

"He sure doesn't belong out there in a Las Vegas parking lot. It's just not natural."

Sears looked around at his men. "I don't suppose Las Vegas is the most natural place in the world for any of us, is it?"

"I don't know," Sonny said. He looked down. There was a smudge left on his belt buckle. He hooked his thumbs over the buckle and covered it with his hands. It wasn't the smudge he was trying to cover. He knew that. "Sticking him on a stage with a bunch of chorus girls . . ." He could feel the executives bristling. They were nervous, worried, wondering what he was going to say next. But Sears retained his poise.

"It's a *wonderful* promotional device," he assured Sonny warmly.

A heavyset woman held a glossy photograph up to Sonny. "Mr. Steele, would you sign this, please . . . 'To Tommy.'"

Sonny took the publicity still, out of habit, and began to autograph it. He stopped suddenly. "No!" he said, abruptly returning the pen she'd given him. The woman glared, then walked away.

"What's a horse got to do with chorus girls?" he asked Sears. The woman had broken through his polite veneer. His anger began to spill out. "What's me acting like an idiot got to do with cereal?"

The men around Sears straightened abruptly. Their shallow smiles disappeared. Dietrich took a step forward. "Just a minute, Mr. Steele," he growled.

"I'm talking to *him!*" Sonny said.

The expression on Sears' face hadn't changed at all. "It sells it, apparently," he responded.

They were looking at him as if he were a rabid dog. All except Sears. Sears was still smiling benevolently. There was the slightest change in his eyes. Behind the wire-rimmed glasses, his cold eyes sparked briefly with amusement and contempt. But Sonny couldn't be sure if he was reading the man right. Frustrated, he clung to the hope that Sears was trying to understand him, that he had started out too hot under the collar, and that if he could just explain himself . . . "Listen," he tried again, "I used to rodeo. . . ."

That's why you hired me. . . . I was pretty good at it."

"What is it, Sonny? What's bothering you? Let's be specific. Is your salary satisfactory?"

"My salary . . . ?"

Sears moved in vigorously. "Is it the amount agreed upon? Is it paid promptly . . . ?"

"I'm not talking about salary . . . I'm talking about feeling like Liberace—light bulbs all over me . . . riding toy horses . . . When I was in rodeo . . ."

"But you're not anymore—"

Sonny looked up. The smile on Sears' face was gone.

"And, actually, you're more famous now, aren't you?" he continued. His smile was gone and his lips were thin and bloodless; they hardly moved when he spoke. His chiseled features seemed suddenly skeletal. "Your face is on millions of boxes, on billboards all over the country. People want your autograph . . ."

"But I don't know where I am half the time."

"If you'd stay more . . . *alert*," Sears said, staring hard at Sonny, making certain that Sonny understood that Sears was a gentleman and that what he'd meant, of course, was sober, not alert. Alert was kind. "Well, then, you wouldn't have those problems."

"You *know* what I'm talking about."

"What I know is that you voluntarily accepted a highly paid, relatively simple job that more than a handful of cowboys would give their right arm for."

Sonny stared at him for a long moment. "You're right," he said.

"I don't want *just* to be right."

"You want to be right and me to like it?"

Sears smiled again, briefly. "It would be a factor in our working relationship."

Sonny turned and started to walk away.

"Mr. Steele . . . ?" Sears' voice pursued him like an icy wind.

Sonny shook his head and kept on going. "I'm going to think on that factor," he said.

The executive who'd tried to stop Sonny before was embarrassed. "I'm sorry, sir," he told Sears.

"Why?" Sears asked, accepting the glass of Perrier one of the men had fetched for him. "He has a right to say what he wants." He took a sip of the sparkling water. Then he turned to Dietrich. "When this is over," he said quietly, "get rid of him."

Sonny was heading for the door when a dark-haired girl in a skin-tight silver gown spotted him. She slipped away from the man she was with and stepped in front of Sonny, blocking his way. Her body pressed up against his. "Hello, famous cowboy," she said.

She was strikingly beautiful. He didn't know why she'd want to run her tongue over her lips that way, or why she was shoving her hips into his. "I'm Sunny Angel," she said breathlessly.

The way she said it, he felt he ought to have recognized her. He didn't. And he wanted to get out of the overcrowded room fast. He wasn't in the mood for rubbing up against her bones or the flesh she was shining his shirt front with. He tried to sidestep her.

"*Revenge of the Cheerleaders? Stews in Chains?* I seen you ride in Cheyenne," she said. She ran her tongue over her lips again. "You sure stay on a *long* time."

He didn't think he knew the girl, but probably

half the cowboys he'd ridden with did. Some nights that didn't matter. Tonight it did. He nodded at her and moved on toward the door, but the girl raked his shoulder lightly with her nails and moved with him.

"You hate parties, *too* . . ." she purred.

He caught her wrist and held it gently. "No, I like parties—they're hard . . . What I can't stand is things that are easy." He let go of her.

He shouldn't have.

She balled her hand up into a fist and took a long, serious swing at his head. "Why, you arrogant, stuck-up, phony big shot!!" she hollered.

There was a frozen moment when, it seemed to him, the entire room, maybe the whole damned world, spun toward them and gasped. His ears burned red with embarrassment. He reached forward to stop her fist and stepped backward, out of her way. His butt hit the big buffet table. With his hands stretched in front of him, there was nothing he could do to steady himself. His arms made crazy circles in the air, as if he was trying to do the backstroke. Then he fell, full weight, into the canapés.

The table, a large round cloth-covered piece of thin wood sitting on top of a square card table, collapsed under him. Anchovies and eggs flew everywhere, and little cocktail franks wriggled out of their dough blankets. He lay back in the mess with his eyes shut tightly until he heard Leroy's voice shouting: "Wendell, I found Sonny!"

Then he opened his eyes. The first person he saw staring down at him was the rough-tough lady reporter. Her green eyes were wide with alarm. She put her hand over her mouth and burst out laughing.

# 8.

# THE MAIN ATTRACTION

Sonny moved through the casino at a good clip. Pieces of canapé still clung to his shirt. On a whim, he bought himself a handful of chips. He tossed them onto the roulette table and kept on going. Then he stopped suddenly. "Oh, no," he whispered.

The blonde at the slot machine heard him. She turned. "Got a quarter?" she said.

"The check's in the mail, Charlotta. Wendell handles all that, you know that."

"How is ol' Wendell, who can't find a stamp?" Her Southern accent had taken on a brittle edge. She heard it herself and blushed. "Oh, damn it all," she said.

"Please don't start up now!"

She had pale eyes rimmed with dark lashes. They were looking up at him, misting unexpectedly. She blinked her lashes trying to see past the sudden blur. "Well, I *have* to talk to you!" she said with a harshness meant to obliterate the tears. "You know I do," she added softly.

He nodded, defeated, and walked with her toward the bar. Charlotta noticed the mess on his shirt, and that his bad back seemed to be acting up again. She slipped her arm through his. Embarrassed, he pulled away. "Don't," he said.

They took a table at the bar overlooking the casino. "Jack Daniels—beer back," Sonny told the waitress. "Give the lady a Rob Roy."

"Orange ade," she said. "I quit."

When the waitress left, he looked down at his hands. "You'll get your check, Charlotta."

"I don't want to talk about checks!"

"Then what'd you follow me all the way here for?"

"I want you to sign the papers!" New tears sprung to her eyes. She snuffled them back angrily and began to rummage in her purse for a tissue.

Sonny stared at her. He was glad about the orange ade. And the way she looked. She'd put on a little weight, but it was honest weight, not the whiskey bloat that had her all puffed up last time he'd seen her. Which was . . . ? Well, a long time ago, it seemed. She looked more like he remembered now. Angel's face and devil's temper.

He wasn't ready to sign the damned papers. He clasped his hands together to keep from reaching out for hers. "Why don't you come up to the room?"

She stared at him trying to read his intention, then gave up. "No," she said.

"Please . . ."

"Aw, Sonny. Don't you think I saw you try to slip out of here? I left three messages at the desk . . ."

"I never got any messages. Maybe Wendell . . ."

"Wendell, my ass! Sonny, the judge said you had to sign it, and I heard your own damned lawyer tell you to sign it. . . . Aw, baby, don't you ever want to be divorced for real?"

He knew she wasn't wearing the ring. He couldn't remember when he'd seen it last. But he looked at her hand, anyway. "We were never married for real," he said childishly. "How come all of a sudden we've got to be so divorced?"

"*You* were the one who was never married. Have you found someone now to sit up all night because you've got a 'flat tire'? Someone to feed breakfast to a dozen cowboys, except some of them were cowgirls who didn't bother not to look like they'd been in the back seat all night. And them sitting right at my kitchen table and . . ."

"You've got a mean memory, Charlotta. One damned party . . ."

"*One party!* That light-up suit must have given you shock treatments! I'm talking about a lot of flat tires and a lot of back seats."

"And you were in plenty of them, and I don't remember any complaining!" He stopped. His nerves were raw and his back was hurting. This time it was his back, but it might have been his arms or legs or his ass, for that matter. Souvenirs. His body was a broken-down ledger book of every competition he'd ridden in. And here he was sitting across from Charlotta, having to explain himself, excuse himself, listen to what a bad person he'd been. Just like the old days. "Christ," he said, "for a few lousy months I don't intend to pay the rest of my life!"

"Well, that ain't going to be much longer, the way you're living! All you're doing is walking around to save funeral expenses."

"Then smile . . . you'll get my insurance!"

"They canceled your insurance!" she shouted back.

"What?" He stared at her. He saw it was true; she wasn't just being mean now. "Where'd you hear that?" he asked, still unable to believe it.

"I got your medical report." She was steaming, but she must have felt bad, too. She traced a design on the table with her finger as she spoke. "You know what your skeleton looks like in the X-ray pictures? A goddamned junkyard! You couldn't get through an airport metal detector stark naked . . . !"

Her voice was harsh, but she kept staring down, watching her fingers move. She was saying terrible things, but at least she couldn't look him in the eye and say them. That had to count for something, he thought. Not much, but something.

". . . Silver wires holding your arms on, pins in your knees . . . probably got a metal hinge to keep your whatchamacallit from falling off. Every damned bone in your body's been broken except two ribs, and those go if anything else happens."

He was chewing on his mustache again. He shook his head. "Well, I'm riding toy horses now, so you can rest easy."

She was exhausted. "Sonny . . . will you sign the papers?" She leaned on the table. "Just let me go, will you . . . ? Just let me go."

He looked at her a long time. Her hair was long and silken now. Little nose and mouth and great big eyes. Cornflower-blue inside circles so dark it looked like someone had outlined them with a pen "Okay . . ." he said quietly. "Give them to me."

She was surprised. She looked to make sure he wasn't joking, then reached into her purse. She had them with her. She handed him the papers. He didn't bother reading them this time. He just looked for the place he was supposed to sign.

Charlotta reached across the table and pointed to it. "What's in there's real fair, Sonny."

He nodded and signed. He had to initial three more pages. Then he handed back the bunch.

"Thank you," she said. He was already on his feet. "Sonny . . . you okay?"

He nodded at her again, gave a half-wave, and walked away.

When he got upstairs, Leroy was waiting in the room. He took one look at Sonny and backed out of the way. The electric cowboy suit was already laid out on the bed.

"Well . . ." Sonny said quietly. "Aren't you going to help me dress?"

It took an hour. He showered and shaved. Wendell arrived. Leroy and Wendell worked him into his back harness and then into the bright blue shirt and trousers appliquéd with beaded flowers and shimmering golden birds. His hat was decorated, too. Blue with gold piping and lights running around the brim and crown. They brushed his shoulders and the seat of the pants and handed him the cord to test the lights. He did. He was leaving the room when Wendell said, "Ah . . . Sonny, I got to tell you something . . ."

He didn't even turn around. "I know," he said. "I seen her already."

He was the only passenger in the elevator. He stood to one side of the mirrored car, anyway . . . in case the doors opened. He didn't feel like having people gaping at him just yet. The lights in the car were white and glaring. He stared straight ahead at the wall panel, at the floor numbers, and at the emergency button. He held the suit cord in one hand. His other shaped itself slowly into a gun. The barrel was his index finger. He aimed it at the wall panel. He pressed the red emergency button.

The car jolted to a stop. Alarm bells rang from every floor. Sonny stood very still in the glaring white mirrored elevator. He just stood there—a tall, tired, sun-leathered cowboy decked out in a light-up suit—listening to the alarms going off.

Hallie met Bernie outside the Circus Maximus. She was late. "Where's your camera?"

"Give me a break, Hallie . . ."

She shrugged. "Too bad you didn't have it at the cocktail party."

They pushed open the door to the nightclub and gave the maître d' their invitations. The show had started. They were seated opposite one another, at the end of a long narrow table that ran parallel to the stage and at a right angle to the ramp that cut through the center of the room.

"What was that racket before?"

"Guy got stuck in the elevator."

There were about fifty people at the table, all wearing plastic-covered identification tags. The enormous room was nearly wall-to-wall Ampco.

On stage, the Salute to Industry was in progress. Colored lights splashed over scantily costumed chorus girls dancing on pieces of machinery—snowplows, tractors, mowers, ski-mobiles. Behind them the word AMPCO shimmered above the running-horse logo. The gigantic earthmover and its papier mâché hill were set up behind the corporate logo and the smaller machines. The music was loud, up-tempo. Familiar patriotic strains ran through it.

"Sounds like Donna Summers meets John Philip Sousa," Hallie whispered.

Bernie's mouth was agape. "Look at those girls!" he said. There was a happy, hysterical edge to his voice. "What are they *doing* up there?! On machines yet! What's this number called, 'Ampco goes to whore' . . . ?"

"That's very rude," the woman next to Bernie said.

He apologized.

Backstage, a second troop of girls was changing for the Ampco fashion show. Racks of costumes lined one wall. Flats on which landscapes of the four seasons were painted were stacked behind a row of gleaming motorcycles. Stagehands were preparing props for the next number. Danny Miles moved past them all to the area where Rising Star was being saddled.

"Is he here? Has anyone seen Steele?"

The wrangler shook his head. Miles threw up his hands and rushed away to supervise the transition between numbers. A few minutes later, Sonny walked in.

He looked very calm, oblivious to the backstage chaos and in no particular hurry. He was wearing the outlandish cowboy costume. The light cord was hooked around his belt. He was dressed and ready, and there was nothing apologetic or hang-dog about the way he carried himself. He headed directly for Rising Star.

The wrangler who was gentling the horse was impressed. He wondered for a moment if Sonny Steele was "on something." Not the juice—he'd heard about that. Steele wasn't moving like a drunk. Just the opposite. He was steady, cool, and deliberate. He seemed very different from the frustrated, angry man who had examined Rising Star earlier in the evening. He seemed self-possessed, in command, and, at the same time, under the control of an outside force, which he either trusted or had no will to fight. That was the puzzling part. That was what suggested the possibility of drugs to the wrangler. Or some fanatical religious experience.

"He's all set, Mr. Steele," the wrangler said.

Sonny looked the horse over. He knelt to examine the game tendon again. He checked the saddle and stirrups and the leather collar, decorated with light bulbs, that ran around Rising Star's neck and over his chest.

Danny Miles returned. "Well . . . Mr. Steele," he said sarcastically.

Sonny ignored the director. He took a step back from the stallion and studied him with quiet admiration. Then he moved over to where he could see the stage. He watched the performers for a moment. He looked thoughtful, then decisive. He turned and walked back to Rising Star, swung himself up into the saddle, and took the reins from the wrangler.

"After this number . . ." Miles held his folded glasses up to his eyes. He glanced at the cue sheet. ". . . then the motorcycle daredevils—God save us—and then you and the horse."

But Sonny had begun moving Rising Star toward the stage. Danny Miles looked up. He watched, first puzzled, then alarmed, as Sonny plugged into the hidden battery pack. Horse and rider were suddenly aglow. The hundred bulbs that traced Sonny Steele's outline blazed fiercely. Rising Star's harness shuddered with light.

"Not *now* . . . !" Miles hollered as Sonny led the stallion onto the stage. "Steele! No, not now!"

It was too late. With the same calm resolution that had impressed the wrangler, Sonny rode Rising Star to the center of the stage. The audience noticed him first. It was their surprise and excitement that cued the performers.

Unsure about whether there'd been a last-minute change in the show, the dancers tried to ignore him. The girls continued to dance; the colored lights washed over the stage; the music faltered momentarily, then picked up again. And Sonny rode slowly, deliberately, down the middle of the stage to the head of the ramp.

The audience was delighted. They jabbered and pointed and some got to their feet to applaud. The woman next to Bernie was one of them. "Oh!" she breathed. "It's so . . . *majestic!*"

And it was, Hallie thought, puzzled. Steele had managed to turn a humiliating stunt into a truly exciting theatrical moment. It wasn't just the quality of the magnificent animal he rode that lent drama and dignity to the performance; it was something about Steele . . . the way he sat, the way he controlled the stallion. There was no high-stepping or galloping or phony rearing up to strike a cereal-box pose. Horse and rider silhouetted in light had become a single awesome apparition.

The stage show behind them was capitulating. But the audience ignored the distintegrating performance as Sonny rode down the ramp through the center of the room. The maître d' at the door watched in disbelief as the vision approached him. Nobody had told him about this part of the show.

"Well?" Sonny said to him quietly. "Open the door."

The maître d' hesitated, then pushed open the doors. "Sorry, Mr. Steele," he said, respectfully, "they didn't say anything . . ."

The people at the dollar slots outside the nightclub stopped pumping the arms of the machines they were playing. They turned in awe and pleasure to watch Sonny's triumphal ride through the casino. The gamblers on the high stools around the blackjack tables laid down their cards to applaud. The roulette wheels slowed. Women in evening gowns around the elegant baccarat tables rushed to the railing to cheer him on.

Sonny felt Rising Star's excitement and held him back, forcing the racehorse to walk in an important, stately way right through the middle of the pit. All around them, gamblers, dealers, waitresses, and pit bosses reacted as the audience in the Circus Maximus had. They gaped, pointed, and cheered with delight.

Through the casino to the front lobby to the glass-enclosed hotel entrance, where two startled tourists held open the doors for them, Sonny Steele and Rising Star moved with dignity inside their circle of constantly twinkling lights. The car-parkers and majordomo watched them come out of the hotel, pause for a second, and then continue riding—picking up the pace now, toward the street.

A bewildered man in the parking lot rushed up to one of the attendants. "Did you see that?!"

The hotel's majordomo glanced over at the empty corral and then back at the glowing silhouette heading for the strip. "Must be *some* breakfast food," he said.

They watched the cowboy in the flashing electric suit, astride the loping thoroughbred stallion, merge with the million lights of Las Vegas, and disappear into the night.

There was bedlam backstage. Chorus girls trooped, bewildered, through the wings, covering their ears against the sound of revving motorcycles. A frantic Danny Miles shouted above the deafening roar, "Forget the routine! Do the finale first!" Someone grabbed his arm. "Get your hands off me!" he shrieked. "Can't you see—" He whirled to face a confused and angry Dietrich.

"What the hell's going on?!" the apoplectic executive demanded. "Why'd you change . . . I mean, what's Steele doing with the horse?"

Danny Miles whipped off his glasses. "What are *you people* doing with Steele!??"

Dietrich spun on his heels and hurried away. He almost collided with Hallie and Bernie in his rush to get to the elevators. Hallie sped through the casino with Bernie in tow. "Don't say it, don't say it . . ." the cameraman urged.

She couldn't restrain herself. Streaking toward the elevator bank, she shouted to him without turning. "Do you know what that footage could have been worth . . . ? One shot of him going through that door . . . ?"

"Oh, shit," Bernie said. "Here comes Boyd."

"Hi. What's the excitement?" Templeton asked.

"Hey, hold the elevator, will you . . . *please* . . ."

But Dietrich disappeared behind the closing doors, and the WBC team watched the floor numbers light up, one by one, all the way to the executive penthouse.

It was a solemn gathering in Sears' suite. Dietrich joined Toland in pacing the length of the sitting room, while a third executive helped Hunt Sears pack. Fitzgerald was staring out the window. He slipped a Gelusil into his mouth and hid the rest of the packet nervously. Sears liked his people lean with nerves of steel. Fitzgerald's nerves were lean. The steel seemed to have settled in his stomach for now.

Danny Miles entered the suite. He'd brought Rising Star's wrangler with him for the command performance. The executive who was helping Sears pack summoned the stoic wrangler into the bedroom. Minutes later, Sears, his tan burnished with rage, stalked out and accosted Dietrich.

"Hunt, it's done all the time. . . ." Dietrich wailed when the Ampco chairman ended his angry monologue. "The tranquilizers keep him calm. The Butazoladine was for the tendon. . . ."

The phone rang again. Fitzgerald, who was already talking on one phone, reached over and answered the other. "Mutual Indemnity and the Nevada State Police—which do you want?" he called out.

"Neither!" Sears spun toward him. "I want this kept quiet."

Fitzgerald nodded. "Like World War Two?" he murmured.

"You might as well know the rest, Mr. Sears,"

said the wrangler. "That cowboy knows horses. I think he guessed we were using steroids to muscle him up."

"Are they dangerous?" Sears asked impatiently.

"Well . . . they make the horse sterile."

"Temporarily!" Dietrich shouted. "It's just a side effect."

Sears was too angry to speak. He just glared at them. "Ah," Danny Miles sighed. "The world of illusion."

Sears sat down. He lowered his head and clasped his hands. "You understand," he began with controlled fury, "this is like handling a loaded gun to Unibank. We're not talking about a horse, gentlemen. We're talking about blowing a three-hundred-million-dollar merger! If Steele talks to *anyone* before he's caught, we're finished. Ampco and the horse are the *same thing!* If we've mismanaged the horse, then we've mismanaged the corporation . . . our stock goes down, and there goes the merger!"

"Couldn't Steele have just called the A.S.P.C.A.?" Fitzgerald said.

Dietrich shot him a silencing look. "What do you want to tell the reporters?"

"To go back to bed," said Sears.

"I don't think that's possible . . ."

"One drunken cowboy!" Sears shook his head in disbelief.

Outside the suite, the reporters were waiting. Fitzgerald had asked the hotel to provide them with free drinks, snacks, coffee . . . anything they wanted to keep them happy while he figured out how best to handle the situation. He opened the door now. They moved in on him like a pack of hungry wolves.

Fitzgerald tried to smile. "Hey, guys, there's nothing I can . . ."

"Is this your stunt, Fitz?" one of them called out to him.

"Seriously, fellers . . . nothing I can tell you now. I don't know any more . . ."

"Did he steal the horse?"

". . . than you people know."

"You look upset, Fitz. Do you have insurance?"

"We won't need insurance!" he barked.

"Oh, I see," Hallie said. "It's just his regular midnight ride on the strip, right, Fitzgerald?"

"Look, if there's anything more to say, we'll see you in the morning. Please, now, you guys . . . and *ladies* . . . restraint. Restraint, huh? I'm going to bed. I suggest you do the same." He pushed past them. A few reporters followed him down the corridor. The rest, after comparing notes and speculation, dispersed.

Hallie returned to her room. She paced back and forth for a few minutes. She began to unbutton her high-necked blouse. Then, abruptly, she hurried to the desk where her tape recorder and note pad rested. She snapped open the flap of the machine's leather carrying case and took the recorder, and a cigarette, with her to the carpeted platform. She sat down on the thick piling and leaned her back against the bed. She stared at the tape recorder for a while. Then she set it down beside her, tapped her teeth with the filter end of the cigarette, and pressed down the "start" button.

She listened to Wendell's voice, and her own:

"That's a very unusual watchband . . ."

"Thank you, ma'am. It's Indian . . ."

She got up while the tape played and walked

back to the desk. She looked for her glasses, found them, and put them on. The Polaroid lenses adjusted to the indoor light. She lit the cigarette, poured herself a drink, and unbuttoned her skirt.

". . . and then when Sonny's daddy, old Shelton, died, Gus raised him. Sonny was married right in Gus' living room . . ."

Hallie sat down at the desk and pulled a number of eight-by-ten publicity stills out of the press folder Ampco had provided. She discarded the photographs of Bud Broderick, Joanna Camden, and General Braithwaite. There were several different shots of Sonny. She flipped through them slowly.

". . . ever a man loved a man, Sonny surely loved Gus Atwater."

Most of the photographs of him were what she expected, ordinary empty-looking glossies: an autographed shot of him atop a rearing horse; a studio still of Steele all lit up holding a glowing box of cereal; Sonny Steele flashing his famous champion's grin. . . . Only one interested her. It was more candid than the others. In it, Sonny appeared to be off guard, unaware that his picture was being taken. Something vulnerable, troubled, showed through.

"And when that woman quit him," Wendell's voice continued, "you know where Sonny came to cool himself out. 'Course, Gus is getting old and strange these days."

"Why'd she quit him?"

"Who knows . . . ? Sonny may have been in the public eye, but he always keeps his private life private. . . ."

The tape ran out. Hallie switched off the machine. She carried the recorder back to the desk

and laid it down next to the special photograph
of Sonny Steele. She was tired. She looked out the
window. There was a big moon tonight. She could
see the mountains far off in the distance. She
half-expected to see a horse and rider outlined in
lights moving along one of the crests.

## 9.

# WILD BLUE YONDER

The first rays of sun sparkled across the vastness of the desert floor. Curled up in a tight ball under a small cluster of trees, Sonny opened one eye. The dawn light hurt. He blinked, stared, saw the expanse of sand, and then the legs of the horse. He squinted up at the animal, then moaned.

He had a terrible hangover. Everything hurt. With great effort, he got to his knees. Wincing, he crawled the few feet to where Rising Star stood and gently examined the swollen tendon on the horse's back leg.

"Goddammit," he said. His voice was thick, still asleep. "Sorry about last night," he told the horse.

Sonny creaked to his feet. Squinting, he searched the horizon. The helicopters that had swooped past like giant insects last night were nowhere to be seen. He remembered how their powerful spotlights had panned the desert floor and how good it had felt afterward to ride out in the clear, cold desert night; to move, he and Rising Star, like shadowy ghosts under the moonlight.

He scanned the horizon and got his bearings. Then he put the saddle on the stallion, fastening it loosely, and took the reins in his hand. "Come on, junkie," he said, leading the horse away from the stand of trees. "We've still got some ground to cover."

He clucked at the horse as they walked, and told him what they were going to do. He wasn't all that sure himself until the words came tumbling out. He told the horse that the first thing they were going to do was visit an old buddy, get some food and some clothes, and, if they were lucky, they'd be able to borrow a camper so that Rising Star could ride in style and get the hell off that bad leg. He apologized but said he stood firm on the fact that the junkie'd have to go straight now. No more of those pain-killers or any of the other crap they'd been keeping him down with. After all, he explained, he didn't want to be all drugged up around the mares when the time came. He'd want to be spry and healthy when he got a whiff of those fine wild mustangs . . . which was a ways off yet, so not to worry. And speaking of legs, his own were no bargain, either. But they were in it together now, so not to worry . . . not to worry about a thing.

"What'd I tell you?" Sonny said, stroking the stallion's nose. "There it is. Ain't much, but, like they say, it's home."

From the hilltop, they looked down at the small cabin. It had a broken-down porch and ramshackle shed in back. Parked awkwardly beside the shed was a handsome Tioga Camper. Its wheels were thick with baked mud that had splashed up onto the body of the van and settled in odd patterns of rusty color over the blue and white frame. But it was new and serviceable. The legend WILD BLUE YONDER was painted across the spare tire. Scrawny chickens pecked and squawked in the shade of the camper. They seemed to be dancing to the faint strains of a squeaky fiddle.

"That'll be him," Sonny said. And despite the sweat, dust, and pain, the trace of a smile began to light his weary face.

Dietrich stepped up to the dais. This time he didn't bother to smile. He didn't even bother to look up at the roomful of reporters and news cameramen. He stared down at the white paper in his hand, and when he heard the drone of the first camera, he turned toward it and began to read.

"We have been advised by the attorney general of the state of Nevada that the theft of Rising Star is grand larceny, a felony . . ."

"Little touch of irony," Hallie whispered to Boyd Templeton. "He and the cowboy were at opposite ends of the table, right up there, yesterday . . ."

Boyd looked at her expectantly. She shrugged.

"That's it?"

"That's it," she confessed.

"Profound, Hallie." He turned back to Dietrich.

"In the event this proves to be a deliberate act, a felony warrant will be issued for Mr. Steele. At this time, however, our primary concern is the welfare of our horse." He put the paper into his pocket and stepped down from the dais. "Thank you, gentlemen. Mr. Fitzgerald will see that you all get copies of the statement. Thank you. That's all for now." Dietrich hurried from the room.

"You see Fitz anywhere?" Hallie asked.

"He's probably in the bar. That's where I'd be if I was Ampco's public relations man."

"Profound, Boyd. Thanks for the tip." She walked out into the corridor, then headed for the bar. Fitzgerald wasn't there. She stood at the railing that overlooked the vast casino and spotted him at the slot machines.

"Hey, Fitz . . ."

He had a drink in one hand and was feeding the machine from a hatful of quarters with the other.

"Hi," he said morosely. He pulled the arm. The machine clicked and clattered and two quarters fell into the slot.

"Big day for you, huh?" Hallie said.

Fitzgerald fed the two quarters back into the machine.

"About the cowboy . . ."

"There'll be a copy of our statement in your room by three, promise." He pulled the lever again. Noise, then nothing.

"What did he say to Sears at the reception yesterday, Fitzgerald? They were at each other. What was that all about?"

"Give us a break, will you, Hallie?"

"Ransom," she said. "What about ransom?"

Fitzgerald shook his head and pumped three quarters into the machine. "The man's not that crazy."

"Have you thought of brain damage? He's been tossed off a horse enough times."

"So the cowboy's emotionally disturbed. Who isn't?" He tugged the arm of the slot machine again. There was a great clattering in the tray. Fitzgerald didn't bother emptying it. He took three quarters from his profits and fed them back into the machine.

"Are you saying he made a mistake and he'll bring it back when he 'cools out' and returns to his senses?"

"I don't know! Leave me alone—I don't *know* any answers. I don't *know* why he took the horse. I don't *know* from brain damage. I don't *know* from cooling out! Go find some *good* news, will you, Hallie, for Chrissakes!" He pulled the lever down ferociously.

She watched him play for a moment more. ". . . cools out . . ." she recited quietly, ". . . cools out . . . cools out?" Then she whirled quickly and left him there, playing the slots.

She hurried to her room, got out the tape recorder, and pressed the "Rewind" button. She drummed her fingernails on the desk impatiently, then hit the "Play" button. Wendell was in the middle of an anecdote.

". . . he 'Indian-gentled' that horse, and when he was done you could put a baby infant on it. That's when he was about . . . oh, thirteen."

It was the wrong story. Hallie pressed the machine's "Fast Forward," listened to the high scrambled sounds for a moment, then tried "Play" again.

". . . Sonny's daddy, old Shelton, died, Gus raised him. Sonny was married right in Gus' living room. Ever a man loved a man . . . Sonny loved Gus Atwater. And when that woman quit him, you know where Sonny came to cool himself out. 'Course . . ."

"Cool himself out," Hallie repeated. She smiled. "You want profound, Boyd-baby? I'll give you profound!"

Downstairs, in the convention hall, a fashion show was in progress. Mannequins modeling Ampco clothes glided through a staged routine while a soothing voice narrated.

". . . in an exciting 'jockey' motif, constructed of synthetic fiber developed in Ampco's new synthetics laboratories. This revolutionary fiber called AMP-STRAND will outwear even the most durable nylons . . ."

Hallie glanced at the anorexic high-fashion models, then made her way through the crowd to the Ranch Breakfast display that featured the cut-out of Sonny Steele, complete with blinking lights. An Ampco man in an Ampco blazer stood dwarfed between the cut-out and a pyramid of cereal boxes.

"Well, hi, there," he said with toothy enthusiasm as Hallie approached.

"Have you seen Wendell Hixson?"

The man retracted his smile as if it were a limited-use item reserved for customers only. "Saw his sidekick hanging around. I think he's in the bar."

"Thanks," Hallie said. She left the display area.

"An extensive array of rainbow colors with coordinated accessories will be available for mass marketing by early fall . . ." the soothing voice promised.

Leroy was in the casino bar having a drink. He was wearing his Stetson and a creamy-colored, Western-styled suit. Hallie slipped into the seat next to him. He touched the brim of his hat politely.

"Seen Wendell?" she asked.

Leroy turned back to her. This time he took off his hat and the thick black hair he'd water-slicked swung forward to his jawline. He swiped at it with his big hand, trying to get it to stay back. "Oh, God, I haven't seen nobody. Everybody's crazy around here today."

She nodded sympathetically. "Can I buy you a drink?"

"Got one. It's my limit."

"Tell me something—just your personal opinion. Are you surprised he did that?"

"Sonny? Oh . . . Sonny surprises you, all right. Some surprises're bigger than others." He uncoiled his drinking hand from the glass and held it out for her inspection. "Gave me this ring. Just like that one day! Had Wendell's teeth fixed for him." He breathed on the ring and polished it on his sleeve.

"What's your last name?"

"Smitely," Leroy said, staring at her with curiosity.

"Hey!" Hallie snapped her fingers. "You know what—I think we have a mutual friend."

"Oh, yeah? Who's that? Who do we know?"

"Gus Atwater." She stared at him. He seemed surprised.

"I know Gus. You know Gus? How do you know Gus?"

She shrugged it off. "Where's he from, Tuba City?" she asked as if she were trying to remember.

"Nah, hell. He ain't but thirty miles from right here. Up by *Mes*quite." Leroy took a sip of his drink. "Sonny takes care of Gus, too. He give him stuff you wouldn't believe."

"Nice talking to you, Leroy," Hallie said. She hopped off the stool and went to find Bernie.

Her luck held. She located him with one phone call. The cameraman was in his room. On her way up, in the elevator, she rehearsed greetings: Hi, Gus. . . . Howdy, Mr. Atwater. . . . Well, hi, there, Gus. . . . She remembered the tape. Wendell had said that Gus was old and strange these days. Old she could handle. She hoped he wasn't too strange.

Bernie was easy to locate but hard to convince. She stood in the corridor outside his door arguing with him in hushed tones. Once she told him what she wanted—which she'd made the mistake of doing flat out, the minute he opened the door —he not only refused, but he refused to let her into his room.

"I'll have it back in twelve hours, Bernie!"

He shook his head again. "I can't do it. I signed for it. I'm responsible for it. I've got to go with you."

"I can't take you with me!"

"Why? What've you got going . . . ? The union says—"

"*Bernie!*"

"No!"

She took a deep breath. Then she smiled. "Bernie . . . I'm covering the French elections in April. You want to go to Paris in April . . .?"

The blue and white Tioga Camper headed northeast along the two-lane blacktop. Sonny was at the wheel. He was clean and shaved and dressed like a human being again. The only light that shone from him was the glare of the highway off the lenses of his dark glasses.

He heard a heavy wheezing sound from the back of the camper and glanced into the rearview mirror. Then he smiled. Rising Star was standing smack in the middle of the Tioga's living area.

"Didn't I keep my promise?" Sonny said. "Don't you call this riding in style?"

Overhead, a police helicopter was making a low pass over the highway. Sonny heard the noise. The shadow of the helicopter darkened the road just ahead, then swung off to the west. The road was one steady stream of recreational vehicles. Wild Blue Yonder was just one of them. In it, they were as safe as two tourists carrying American Express cheques.

"How's that leg, junkie . . . ? First chance, I'll get you something for it. No more drugs, though. We'll try something natural."

The town was so small, it didn't have a proper name. The store did, though: Celestial Aura Health Food Store.

"I think we hit pay dirt," Sonny said.

He adjusted his dark glasses, pulled his hat down low over them, and, for good measure, tossed a blanket over his shoulders. He was a walking disguise when he crossed the dusty main street and stepped into the small, sparkling-clean store.

"Morning," the girl behind the counter said cheerfully. She looked like something out of a picture book of olden days: a pretty little thing in a print dress that came down to her ankles, and wheat-colored hair that hung to her waist.

"Morning," Sonny said. "Have any eucalyptus leaves?"

"You must be a Capricorn." She seemed pleased.

Sonny stared at her. He licked his bottom lip, then bit his mustache. Then he said, "Ah . . . have any eucalyptus leaves?"

"Just tea bags."

"Well, I need some of them tea bags."

"How many do you want?"

He tugged at the blanket and sniffed authoritatively. "Four or five dozen."

"Four or five dozen tea bags?"

"Boxes," Sonny said.

He tossed the parcels into the camper and scurried in beside them. An hour and a half out of town, he saw the "No Trespassing" sign. He eased the Tioga off the road and drove it through some low-lying brush to a narrow, rocky trail that disappeared behind a high plateau. The plateau was fringed with scrub trees and sweet-smelling sage.

He led Rising Star down a ramp made of planks that Gus had helped him fashion. He left the horse in the shade of the trees while he started up a small fire. Then he tossed a batch of tea bags into the flames and fetched the horse. By the time he'd gotten the gunny sack tied over the stallion's ears, the fire was smoking heavily.

Sonny moved the horse over to the pungent fire. He grasped the bottom of the gunny sack, ripped it open, and made a chimney of it over the smoke. He gentled the horse and held the sack bottom open around the little fire. Now and again, he fed fresh tea bags to the glowing coals.

"Take care of that wheezing, for you. . . . Couple more times, you'll be breathing fine," he said. His own eyes were tearing and his nose smudged and runny from the smoke. He was coughing up a storm. He caught his breath. "Be fine," he promised, ". . . if *I* live. . . ."

The sun was going down when he stomped out the last of the fire. Rising Star was craning his silky neck into the brush, nibbling at the wildflowers and minty sage. Sonny strolled over to him.

"Well, how're you doing now? You like this place, do you? This ain't nothing compared to what's ahead. This is strictly small-time, junkie."

He pulled up a piece of sweet grass and chewed on it. The sky was streaking red and purple. The whole world he looked out on was burnished with the rosy end of day. Just beyond the rise on which he stood were the ruins of an old building or two. Behind one of the crumbling façades, he'd make camp tonight.

He loved this time, this place. It was where he used to come after his daddy died. He'd tell Gus that he was running away from home and the old man would offer him a lift. Gus would pack him a little bag of food with an extra-warm shirt in it. Then they'd climb up into the cab of the pickup truck and Gus would drive him up here. And let him alone for an hour or two.

The "No Trespassing" sign never bothered Gus. He counted it one of the blessings of the place. Kept out the hotheads—boys or men with guns and a mean streak looking for something to kick or shoot.

Sonny knelt and examined the horse's bandaged tendon. He talked softly to calm the animal as he unwrapped the elastic cloth.

"Don't know what was wrong with those people," he said. "Why, you look just fine in that old sock . . . like you're going out to the country club, play a little tennis . . ."

He tightened and fastened the bandage again. Then he led the horse gently over the rise toward the shells of the burned-out buildings.

It must have been near midnight when Sonny heard the car driving in. The sound startled him awake. He'd drifted off to sleep right in the middle of dinner. It was too late to put the fire out now or to hide the horse, tethered nearby. He rolled over and started creeping, moving as far from the cook fire as he could without making noise. As long as the car kept coming, he was covered. When the motor shut off, he'd have to drop, wherever he was.

He worked his way up the hummock and traveled along a ravine on the other side. He saw the car pulling up behind the Tioga. The car was small, white in the moonlight. It idled awhile with its lights on; then the lights died and the motor was switched off. Sonny thought he heard voices coming from the car. One of them had a familiar cadence. It stopped and started, drifted and returned, like Gus's voice. . . .

It was Hallie's tape recorder. The voice did belong to Gus Atwater, but she wasn't playing it for road instructions this time; she was playing it just for the company . . . just because she was scared stiff.

"Golden wheat . . . 'bove her head . . . glimmerrr . . ."

That's what the old man had started singing when he first saw her.

"Mr. Atwater?"

"You wounded?" he'd asked.

"No, but I'm looking for a friend of ours."

"Ain't here." He'd started playing his fiddle again, watching her closely.

"But he was," she'd said.

"Yep, from this high!"

"Was he here today?"

"Here today, gone tomorra' . . ."

"Gus . . . I'm a friend of Leroy's. . . . And Wendell . . . ? They told me you'd know where he was. We're all worried about him. I just want to talk to him . . . I can't hurt him. . . . Is he okay? Where'd he go, Gus?"

Hallie shut off the tape recorder, pulled her knit hat down over her hair, and got out of the car. It was cold out. She was shivering clear through her cute little denim jacket and her expensive designer jeans. Two steps told her the high-heeled boots were hazardous to her health, but she continued on clumsily. She picked her way up the rock-strewn path, hoping that the fat, crunchy things she was stepping on and tripping over had no taste for human flesh, or expensive Italian leather, for that matter.

Her eyes were opened so wide with fear and trying to see in the dark that her forehead seemed to have shrunk. Her hat was eating her eyebrows. She considered calling out to Steele. Anything would be better than butting her head against the wall of icy blackness ahead. She opened her mouth. She barely had time to gasp.

There was a shocking blur of movement. A hand smacked flat against her teeth. It clamped over her mouth, paralyzing her jaw. Her back hit the ground. Her lungs seemed to empty in a great whoosh of air, leaving her aching, breathless, terrified. She had no time to recover. Dead weight landed on her belly. She managed to open her eyes. She closed them quickly, cringing against the balled fist that was aimed at her face.

"Wait!!!" she screamed with all her might. The blow never came. Hallie opened her eyes again. Steele had her pinned to the ground. A look of stunned recognition crossed his face.

She was nearly delirious with relief.

Then he hit her.

Hallie squirmed, gasping. She couldn't feel the side of her face where his hand had landed. It was gone. Then it was back, burning. "Don't . . . please don't—"

"What're you doing?! What do you want? How'd you find me?!"

He had her pinned to the ground. The back of her head ached. Her teeth felt loose. He was shaking her, bumping her head against the rocks and hard earth underneath.

"Please! You're hurting—"

"How'd you find me? Who's with you?"

"I'm alone, I'm alone . . ."

"*Who's with you??*"

"I swear!" He raised his arm again. "I was playing the tape recorder!!" she screamed.

"How'd you get here?!"

"Myself . . . I drove myself!"

"How?" He seized the neck of her jacket and twisted it in his fist. "How'd you *find* me?"

"Gus! Gus Atwater!"

He let go of her. "How'd you get to Gus?" he asked, moving off her slowly.

"Can I get up . . . ? Please."

He backed away a step. "How would you know how to find Gus?"

She sat up. The side of her face was throbbing.

"By accident," she said, touching her cheek gingerly. "I interviewed your friends. I figured—" She got to her knees.

"Who??" he demanded impatiently.

She tried standing. "Wendell . . ." she said, ". . . Leroy . . . they talked about Gus. . . . I . . ." She stopped suddenly, as if she'd just remembered something. Listen, what is it with you? You hit my face, you son-of-a-bitch! What the hell's the matter with you?"

Then she slapped him. Hard.

"I'm not staying here!" she hollered. She turned and started back toward her car. Then she stopped, turned back, and stared at him a moment. "What'd you take the horse for?" she asked.

Sonny stared at her in disbelief. "What are you doing here? You're crazy! Who else knows about Gus?"

"Nobody. Nobody knows about Gus," she said. Then: "*I'm* crazy?! You disappear with somebody's twelve-million-dollar horse, and you call me crazy?"

He moved toward her. "Hold it, hold it, *hold it!*"

"Don't you hit me," she warned.

He began to walk around her, trying to figure out what to do. Hallie kept a wary eye on him as he circled.

"Did you scare that old man?" he asked, more thoughtfully than threateningly.

"No."

"Does anybody else know you're here?"

"I told you nobody knows anything! I don't have any reason to tell anybody anything!"

He stopped, thought, gave her a curt nod of his

head. Then he started up the rise. "Go away," he said tiredly. "Go home."

She dusted off her jeans and jacket and followed him. "What are you going to do with him?"

"There's a dog-food factory in Phoenix," he said. "Go home."

The campfire was visible from the top of the ridge. Sonny made his way back to it. The remains of his dinner lay beside the fire. He crouched down, tossed them out, and began to put away the cooking gear.

Hallie watched him. "Just tell me why you took the horse."

He didn't answer.

"You can't race him, you can't sell him, you can't start your own cereal company. What the hell *do* you want?" Unconsciously, her hand went to her cheek. She winced and pulled it away. "Were you mad at Ampco? I saw you arguing with Sears . . ."

Sonny ignored her. Unhurried and methodically, he gathered up his utensils and carried them from the fire to his saddlebag.

"Were they going to fire you? Did you want a raise . . . ? Can't you just answer a question?!" She stared at his back "Listen," she said after a moment, "I don't have anything against you . . . I mean, I don't usually get slugged doing this, but even so, I—"

"Hell'd you expect?" he said without turning around. "Sneaking upon me like some cat!"

"I tried to call, but your line was busy!"

He spun and looked at her. She couldn't make out the details of his face at a distance, but the set of his head, his body, the sudden movement, silenced her. It was what he wanted. He went back to work, cleaning up.

"Look," Hallie said gently when he returned to the fire, "your friends are worried about you—I mean, Wendell and Leroy. Can I tell them anything?" Her revised tone of voice didn't seem to help much. She was standing halfway up the little hill. She looked around. She was looking for something to say.

"What is this place? Does it mean something to you?" He didn't answer. Well, maybe old Gus would. Or Wendell or Leroy. But not if she filed a story, they wouldn't. Not *when* she filed the story, she amended the thought, because come hell or high water, she was going to do just that. If Sonny Steele wanted to play the strong, silent type, fine. Great, in fact. That would give her more leeway to editorialize, to present her own ideas and impressions. And if he didn't agree with what she said, let him phone the F.C.C. and ask for equal time.

But, damn, she wished he'd talk!

"No messages for anybody, huh?" She thought of the woman in the hotel lobby, the angel-faced blonde with the big bust. Mrs. Sonny Steele. Charlotta. "Somebody you forgot to say good-bye to?"

Nothing. Not even one of those Gary Cooper-type "Nope's"; not a "nope" or a "yup" or a "mebbe." Some cowboy he was! Some reporter she was. . . .

Hallie was tired. Her face hurt. Her mind was closing shop, even if her mouth was still open. And she was cold. She realized that suddenly. She was chilled to the marrow. The wind ripping around Riverside Drive had never reached the depths of deep-down cold she felt right now.

She hurried down the rise and moved over to the fire. She was too cold to stand and too wary of him to sit. So she wrapped her arms around herself and bent toward the flame.

Sonny threw a blanket over Rising Star. Then he, too, moved toward the campfire. There were a few things left to pack. He knelt down and began to gather them together. Then, all at once, he looked up at her.

The firelight lit his pale eyes and wind-blown hair. It threaded golden through his thick mustache. He looked at her, but he didn't see her looking back. He didn't really see her studying his face, recognizing it. It was the same troubled, vulnerable face she'd found among the publicity stills.

"You want information—go to the library," he said. He sounded more tired than angry. He spoke very quietly. "I know what you want, and it's not answers. You want a story. Any story. Why don't you make one up? That's what you'll do, anyway —tell it the way *you* want to tell it. . . ."

She was startled that he seemed to have "overheard" her secret thoughts, and startled, too, because his tired voice had taken on an explosive bitterness. He stood up and stared into the firelight. It made her very nervous. She didn't like it that he was taller than her again; menacing. She hugged herself hard and tried to stand straighter.

"You don't need me to tell you a story! You guys make them up all the time, anyway . . . ! Ask me questions about why I'm forty-five minutes late—you're not interested in why I'm late; all you're interested in is getting a rise out of me! 'Pound for pound, who's worth more, you or the horse?' Who the hell cares? You people are all the same."

She didn't know whether it was fear of him that had her adrenaline pumping again or anger because he was classifying her, trying to pigeonhole her, calling her "you guys" and "you people. . . ." And she was damned if she'd tell him that her private thoughts *were* her private thoughts and she knew, even if he didn't, that it was her actions that counted. . . .

"You know," he said suddenly, "there's people in Africa or some damned place . . . you take a picture of them, they'll kill you. They think you're taking something away from them, that you've only got so much . . . stuff! . . . and if other people are taking it all, then there's none left for yourself. Well, I don't want to be no story. . . ."

He bent to retrieve an old enamel coffeepot that had been sitting on a rock near the fire. He looked up at her again. This time, he seemed really to be looking, to be talking directly to her. "I just retired from Public Life," he said.

"Boy, have you got it wrong! You just rode down the Las Vegas strip on somebody else's twelve-million-dollar horse," she reminded Sonny Steele. "Did you think we wouldn't notice?" *We guys, we people,* she wanted to say. "You're a story, all right."

He poured the remaining coffee onto the fire, putting it out. The embers smoked and hissed in the moonlight. "But not yours," he said, quiet again. "I'm nobody's story but my own now."

He carried the pot with him back to where his saddlebag and Rising Star were waiting. He put the coffeepot away, and untethered the stallion, and led him past Hallie toward the top of the rise. She watched and waited for a moment, then ran after him.

"Wait a minute. Where're you going?"

He kept going.

"Aw, I hurt your feelings. I didn't mean to hurt your feelings." She stumbled after him in the darkness. "Was it something I said . . . ? Come on, do a working girl a favor—I'm trying to make an honest buck. Tell an honest tale, make an honest dollar. I don't want to *make up* a story about you."

He led the horse down the rocky path. Hallie hurried along after them, picking her way over unseen obstacles. She didn't like her positioning in this parade, she thought. But what the hell, it wasn't a man and horse she was following, it was a story. And the story was slipping away. . . .

She called out to Steele again. "What's the big secret? What've you got to lose? Everybody wants to know. They wonder where you are, why you did it . . . where you're going . . . the truth about the Great American Cowboy and the world's champion horse who disappear into the sunset."

"Boy, are you full of shit. With all due respect, ma'am." He'd reached the Tioga. Hallie's rental car was parked behind it. He turned. "And you're standing in poison sumac," he said.

She jumped. She ran out of the clump of bushes, over to the camper, where he was leading Rising Star up the ramp.

"You son-of-a-bitch!" she railed at him. "You're not getting away from me. I'll follow you!"

He finished snapping the chain that braced the horse's buttocks. Then he grabbed a flashlight from the camper, stepped out, and closed the back door. He walked around the camper to

Hallie's car. The keys were in the ignition. He took them, opened the trunk, and took out the spare tire.

"What?" she yelled. "What're you doing??"

He tossed her the flashlight and her car keys, then reached down and pierced her rear tire with the tip of his pocket knife. The tire hissed ominously.

"Shouldn't take you more than twenty minutes," he said.

"Goddamn you! You're nuts! I'll turn you in! I see your license plates! I'll tell the cops, you bastard—Wild Blue Yonder!"

He opened the front door of his camper. "No, you won't," he said calmly. "You're going to milk this story for all it's worth. The last thing in the world you want is for me to be captured. We both know a captured horse thief ain't no story." He was in the Tioga, then gone.

# 10.

# LIVE FROM
# CAESAR'S PALACE

Hallie stood in the parking lot in front of the empty AstroTurfed corral.

"It was from this hotel that Rising Star, the greatest money-winner in the history of American racing—and, presently, corporate symbol for one of the world's largest conglomerates—was taken late Friday night." She faced the bank of cameras, behind which a number of tourists strained to watch the live broadcast.

"She sure wears a lot of makeup," a woman in the crowd whispered to her husband.

"Something wrong with her lips, too. Crooked. Strange how you see someone on TV all the time and their lips move just fine. . . ."

"Yesterday," Hallie continued, "I uncovered information which allowed me to locate Sonny Steele. . . ."

He was in Utah when he caught the show.

He was standing in a small family grocery store staring at his picture on the front of a Ranch Breakfast box. He wore his dark glasses and the blanket and, of course, his hat pulled down low. His arms were loaded with groceries, including the plastic bag of ice he'd bought for the junkie's leg.

He'd just asked the grocer for shoelaces. The man could hardly hear him over the TV's blare. His little girl was watching cartoons and the sound was way up.

"Shoelaces," Sonny repeated.

"Anita!" the grocer hollered at the child. "Get rid of that stuff!"

But the kid was transfixed. With an angry sigh, the grocer went to change the channel himself. "Over there by the shoe polish," he told Sonny.

While the man changed the station, Sonny got the laces, then walked toward the counter with his purchases. Hallie's face flashed on the screen just as he got to the counter. He almost dropped the groceries. He ducked his head and started digging for his money, fast.

". . . there by the dim glow of a shrouded campfire, I saw Rising Star and encountered Sonny Steele himself. We talked together for hours. . . ."

*"Whaat??!"* Sonny said.

The grocer looked over at him. "What?"

Sonny turned to the man. "What?" He slapped his money onto the counter and lowered his head again.

". . . as a result of our wide-ranging conversation, I formed these impressions—" Behind Hallie, a huge blow-up of Sonny suddenly occupied the screen.

He ignored his change and headed for the door. Hallie's voice pursued him.

"Steele, in my opinion, did not take the horse for monetary gain. He has no intention of ransoming Rising Star. . . ."

"Well, how was it? How'd the makeup look?" Hallie asked Boyd Templeton. She signed another autograph on her way back into the hotel.

"Great, and not so great—in that order."

But he held the door open for her and said, "Thanks, folks. That's enough for now. Miss Martin's had a long night, as you all know. No more autographs. Thank you."

Fitzgerald was rushing out of the elevator as Hallie and Boyd were moving toward it. He hurried up to them. "Hallie, can I see you a minute?"

"I've got to take this crap off," she said, touching her cheek inadvertently as she pointed to the makeup. She tried to turn the grimace into a quick smile.

"Can you come up to Sears' suite in, say, fifteen minutes . . . alone, please?"

"Why, Fitz," Boyd said, "that sounded positively indecent."

"Probably is," Hallie decided in the elevator. "But I wouldn't miss it for the world."

"Tell me the truth, Hallie—did he slug you?"

"Oh, Boyd, really!"

Les Charles, WBC's news director, phoned from New York while Hallie was refilling the ice pack.

"How'd you like the broadcast, Les?" She stuck her tongue out at Boyd. "Oh, thanks . . . right. Thanks . . . oh, well, shucks . . . just doing my job. Yeah, well, thanks. It did? Oh, shit! Listen,

I'll tell you about that another time, okay? Glad you called. Bye."

"What'd he say?"

"All the right things," Hallie said.

"And one wrong?"

"He said my face looked lopsided. I'm going up to see Sears now. Alone."

Dietrich opened the door to the penthouse. Fitzgerald offered Hallie a drink. Toland gave her his seat on the sofa and peered at her disapprovingly through his wire-rimmed glasses. Sears, sitting opposite, said, "Where is he?"

"I don't know."

"Where was he?"

"I don't know."

Sears smiled his thin-lipped smile and glanced at Fitzgerald.

"What did he tell you, Hallie?" Fitzgerald asked.

"Nothing."

Sears nodded slowly. He looked to Toland, who was grim-faced and steely eyed, then back to Hallie.

"Miss Martin . . ." It was Dietrich's turn. "If you want a story, we could put you in the middle of a story. . . . We *could* guarantee you first crack at everything."

"I've already had first crack at everything."

"Suppose we made it exclusive?" Fitzgerald was back in the game. "How about if we gave you exclusive footage on the capture?"

"Oh? When are you planning that?" She tried to smile. It hurt. She looked back at Sears. "You want to tell me about that confrontation you and Steele had at the reception, Mr. Sears? What was that all about?"

Sears made a steeple of his fingers. "We could, Miss Martin, take you to court."

"You could try."

Toland took off his glasses and pinched the bridge of his nose. "Aiding a felon during the commission of a felonious act . . ." His eyes were closed. He seemed to be reciting to himself. "Concealment of a felony . . . mis-prison of a felony . . ." He opened his eyes and stared directly at Hallie. "That's what the law calls it."

"Well . . . you aren't the law, but if Ampco wants to challenge the First Amendment, be my guest." She stood. "That ought to sell America a whole lot of breakfast food." She walked to the door of the suite. "I'll be around, if you want to handcuff me later," she said, then left.

Sears stared at the closed door.

"We could probably take her to court," Toland said.

Dietrich tapped his breast pocket, looking for his silver pencil. "Hell, we could have her locked up."

"The last thing we need now is a female martyr. . . . No." Sears' voice was still silky. He glanced at Toland again.

"I wonder if she'll see him again," Dietrich mused.

"Is she being watched?"

"Already taken care of," Toland assured Sears.

"How did she find him?"

"At least he didn't say we mistreated the horse."

Sears raised his eyebrows at Dietrich. "How do we know that?"

Fitzgerald answered. "I think she'd have said it on the air."

"You think?"

"Well . . ."

"That's not a chance we can afford to take," the Ampco chairman said.

"Do we have a choice?"

Sears pinned Fitzgerald with an icy glare. "We have to make sure that if he does say anything, he won't be believed. Can you get to the media before the eleven o'clock news?"

The mountains of southern Utah were snow-capped. A cold mountain stream reflected the last rays of sun. In the waning light, Sonny worked on Rising Star. He'd cut the leg off a pair of old pants and slipped it over the horse's rear leg. Now, he tied the bottom closed with one of the shoe-laces he'd bought in the store where he'd caught the tail end of Hallie's broadcast.

The stallion shuddered. Sonny gentled him, clucked to him, and fetched the plastic bag of ice from the stream. He filled the pants leg with ice and tied the top closed with the other shoe-lace. Satisfied, he settled under a tree for a nap.

He lowered his hat over his face, then lifted it abruptly and looked at his watch. "Damn," he said. He'd missed the evening news. He'd intended to listen on the Tioga's radio, see if Hallie Martin was shooting off her mouth again. He shook his head just thinking about all that business she'd invented. Then he smiled. Shooting off *half* her mouth, he reminded himself. The other half didn't appear to be working all that well.

He only managed a short nap. It started to rain. He loaded Rising Star back into the camper, climbed into the driver's seat, and hit the road again.

Nightfall made him feel safer, at least about

picking up a cup of coffee at a truck stop. The rain helped, too. Every reason in the world to throw a blanket over your shoulders on a cold and rainy night. He kept his head down when he paid the cashier and scooted across the road to where the Tioga was parked in the shadows away from the big rigs.

Rising Star was standing in the back; his eyes were closed. Sonny tore a half-moon out of the plastic cover on the Styrofoam container and put the lid back on the steaming coffee. He took a sip through the mouthpiece he'd fashioned, then got the camper back on the road. He switched on the radio for some stay-awake country music. Every couple of miles, he'd check on the horse in the mirror. The rain was good for getting coffee in, but worrisome and monotonous to drive through.

"If I could drive sleeping the way you can sleep standing," he told the stallion, "why, we'd have this thing knocked."

The country tune ended. "It's ten-fifty-nine here at KLSG in St. George and time for the eleven o'clock news roundup. Here is Harvey Del Rio for Rudolph Brothers Lumber and Building Supplies. Harvey."

The windshield wipers flapped at the rain. Sonny turned up the radio a touch.

"Thanks, Clayton." The voice of Harvey Del Rio was uneven, punctuated with static. "Retail sales clerks are on strike in Salt Lake. Union officials in the . . . prepared to walk out in sympathy . . . Vegas, investigators still have no . . . to the whereabouts of Rising Star, the great . . . whose abduction by Sonny Steele Friday . . ."

Sonny turned up the volume and fiddled with the dial. He listened intently.

". . . massive search. Ampco officials are now expressing alarm over the welfare of the horse. According to one . . . 'eele has a long history of alcoholism and drug abuse . . ."

Sonny slammed the dashboard above the radio with his palm. The static cleared. ". . . appeared before the public in an intoxicated state on several occasions, and has been abusive to both press and public. Ampco officials indicate he has become increasingly unstable, often causing public humiliation. They believe that if the horse is to survive this ordeal, time is of the essence."

Sonny snapped the radio off. He checked his watch, then looked back at the road. There wasn't another town or truck stop in sight. Sooner or later there would be. They were right about one thing—time was of the essence. He hoped it'd be sooner than later.

Cleopatra's Barge seemed to have been commandeered by the press. A dozen or so of the reporters covering the convention were having nightcaps in the bar. Hallie was the center of their attention. Bernie sat beside her; Fitzgerald sat opposite.

"You're hot, Hallie." One of her colleagues tipped his glass toward her. "Christ, they'll be calling on you to find lost kids next."

"Fitz," she asked, "who wrote that crap about him?"

"That 'crap,' " Fitzgerald insisted, "is all true."

"What's this bozo's plan? What do you think he's going to do?" another reporter asked.

"What's *your* next move?" Fitzgerald looked at Hallie.

She shrugged. "It's *your* convention."

"Come on, this is serious. Give us a hint."

Hallie had some idea which "us" he meant. "How's your dog, Fitz?"

"His dog died," a young reporter said.

The man who'd told Hallie they'd be calling on her to find lost kids shook his head incredulously. "Some guy out there won four hundred thousand bucks in seven hours. Can you believe it?!"

Fitzgerald stretched languorously. "I can believe it. I saw him lose half a million."

Bernie was yawning. "Where's the camera?" he asked Hallie.

"My room."

"Hallie . . . Hallie . . ." One of the guys breathed bourbon into her face. "You never saw the joker. C'mon. Admit it."

Someone came over to Fitzgerald and waved an itinerary sheet in front of him. "What is this ten o'clock in the morning with golf balls?"

"We make golf balls."

"Hallie . . . Hallie . . . if you were there, you would never have left him."

"She leaves everybody," someone said.

"Yeah, but not a story like this."

"Give, Martin. He must have told you something!"

"Yup," she said. "He told me what was wrong with the press." She finished her drink. "I got a lecture on morality from a horse thief."

"What's he want? Where did he go?"

Hallie stood. "It's our secret. Night, guys. Keep your nose clean, Bernie."

"You're really loving this, aren't you?" Fitzgerald said.

She patted his cheek and left the bar. She was passing the casino area on her way to the elevators. The late-night shooters and rollers leaned quietly into their games. An overly made-up woman stood alone at the roulette wheel. The blackjack tables were relatively still; two or three people per, where usually the stools were fully occupied and kibitzers stood two deep.

A weary-looking blonde swept her chips from one of the horseshoe-shaped tables into her purse. She spotted Hallie and hurried across to her. "Pardon me, Miss Martin."

Hallie turned.

"I'm Charlotta Steele."

"Oh . . . hello."

"I was married to Sonny," the woman said shyly.

"Yes," Hallie said. She smiled. She tried to smile warmly but objectively. Fascinated, she tried to disguise the personal curiosity that had unexpectedly allied itself to her professional interest. "I know," she said.

"I didn't mean to take your time—"

"It's all right."

"I was going to drive home," Charlotta Steele said. "But then he went and did what he did. . . . I was just wondering if he was all right. He isn't hurt?"

"No."

She ran a hand through her straight hair, then curled a lock of it around her index finger. "Are you going to see him again?"

"We didn't make any plans. Why?"

"Just wondering."

And worrying, Hallie thought, studying the woman. Her eyes were very large and blue. Very beautiful eyes, really. And troubled now. "Why

do you think he did it?" Professional curiosity
had won out and she was pleased.

"I don't know. . . . He gets ornery . . . and it
takes a long time sometimes for him to admit he's
got a horn in his gut."

"What's the horn in his gut, Mrs. Steele?"

"All's I know, he must have had a reason, else
he would have been back by now. He's not a
thief by nature. I mean, he takes your breath,
but . . ." She looked at Hallie suddenly, then
looked away, shy again. "They only said those
bad things about him. They didn't say what's de-
cent . . . even though it's hard to find it sometimes."

"You found it, didn't you?" Hallie said gently.

"For a while." She had run out of talk. "I want
you to know I . . . I really enjoy watching you on
TV."

"Thank you," Hallie said. She wasn't ready to
end the meeting yet. "How did you meet Sonny?"

Suddenly, Charlotta laughed raucously. Hallie
was impressed. The woman was obviously delighted with the memory.

What he'd found and settled on, after a couple
of hours, was a dingy juke joint off the highway.
He pulled the Tioga around to the dark side of
the place, put on his glasses, hat, and the blanket,
and walked inside. Country music was blaring
from the jukebox. There were a few late-night
truckers having a beer. He ordered one at the bar,
then crossed to the pay phone on the wall.

"Hallie Martin, please," he said when the hotel
operator got on the line.

She picked up on the second ring. "Who the

hell . . ." he heard her grumbling sleepily. Then: "Hello?"

"You alone?" His whispering voice was low and gravelly.

"Who's this?"

"You alone?"

She sighed. "Okay, feller, say your dirties and get it over with."

"I think it's time for another 'wide-ranging conversation,'" he said.

She almost dropped the phone. He could actually hear the sheets rustling as she sat up.

"Hello?" he said.

Finally, she found her voice. "Is this you?"

"Right out of the 'dim glow of the shrouded campfire. . . .'"

"You bugger, I broke three nails changing that tire!"

"Do you want a story?"

That got her. She caught her breath and said, "Yes."

"Can you get out of there without anybody knowing?"

"Yes. If I can't, I won't come."

He hesitated.

"Tell me where to go," she urged.

"You're going to start with a bus . . ."

She reached down beside the bed for her pad and pen. "Yes," she said, "go on. . . ."

After he hung up, Hallie scooted out of bed and began to dress. There wasn't a thing she could do about the boots. They were the most 'sensible' shoes she'd packed. But she remembered the cold. She took a quick look at the clock, then phoned down to the desk. By the time the bell captain knocked at her door, she was fully dressed and ready.

"Gary, I have to get out of here without being seen." She handed him the money. "It's worth a hundred dollars."

He smiled. "All things are possible, Miss Martin. Follow me."

"I've got a couple of cases inside. Could you grab them?" she asked.

The bell captain put the money away, then followed her into the room.

# 11.

# FUGITIVES

Outside the hotel, workmen were dismantling Rising Star's corral: carting off the plastic logs and rolling up the AstroTurf. Inside, another group of workmen swarmed over the convention area. A few of them carried the oversized cut-out of Sonny away from the Ranch Breakfast display booth. A janitor swept up behind them. He pushed the tangle of wires that had connected the cut-out's lights onto the pile of rubbish that his assistant was bagging.

Wendell and Leroy watched the men. Leroy shook his head sadly.

"She acted like my best friend," he said suddenly.

Wendell nodded.

"She wanted to buy me a drink . . . she even liked my ring."

"Sonny and I told you—never trust those people," Wendell said with a hint of impatience. "She liked my watch. . . . I liked her eyes. . . . That's what they do—act like they're your best friend, then use you." He sighed. "Let's get out of here. Go sit by the pool or something. . . . You seen that broadcast," he said as they walked to the lobby. "She's using him just like she used us."

"What're we going to do?"

"Nothing," Wendell said definitively. "If he wanted us to do something, he'd let us know." They made their way through the casino toward the elevators. "I liked her eyes," Wendell said.

Fitzgerald hurried past them. He pressed the "Up" button and paced nervously in front of the elevators.

"Morning," Leroy said.

Fitzgerald nodded at them. The light above one of the elevators went on, and the doors opened. He rushed into the car and pressed the "Penthouse" button. A waiter with a breakfast cart was just leaving Sears' suite. Fitzgerald waited until the man maneuvered the cart into the corridor. Then he went inside.

"Who saw him?" Sears was asking.

"Some little shopkeeper in southern Utah," Dietrich replied. "Near St. George, yesterday. He must have gotten a vehicle."

Toland was on the phone. He covered the mouthpiece. "He's evidently been heading northeast. If he stopped for the night, he should be within one hundred fifty miles of St. George."

"Who knows about this?"

"The local police are all taken care of," Dietrich said. "Nobody else."

"The press?" Sears turned to Fitzgerald.

"Not yet."

"All right, take care of it," Toland spoke into the mouthpiece.

"Can we get to the surrounding towns in time?" Sears asked him.

"I'm handling that right now. They think we should concentrate on Hurricane, Liberty, and Cedarville."

"All right. You and Toland get on the Lear, right away," Sears instructed Dietrich. "Take the security people with you. You can organize everything out of St. George."

"*If* he stopped for the night."

Dietrich glared at Fitzgerald. "We've got to assume he sleeps sometimes!"

"He's crossed the state line," Toland said. "The F.B.I. will want in."

"Can we keep them out?"

"They already know he's been spotted. They'll be crawling all over the place."

"Get to him first!" Sears said. "Offer him whatever you have to. Tell him we won't prosecute. Do what you have to do. Just don't let him utter any nonsense about the horse. Let's put this together and get the damned thing done with!"


Hallie drove along a stretch of empty highway. She'd rented the car in St. George, as Steele had said to do. She'd done everything exactly as he'd instructed. Now all she had to do was find the dirt road. She looked at the speedometer and checked the mileage. Either she'd passed it, or it would be coming up on the left any minute now.

She slowed down. It was a good thing, too. A car preceded by two motorcycle cops appeared out of nowhere. She thought she saw the road up ahead. She'd already decided not to turn onto it with the police so near when the motorcade passed her and disappeared around a bend in the highway. She drove on, anyway. After a few solitary miles, she made a U-turn and drove back to the dirt road.

The Tioga was parked where he said it would be. Hallie pulled up alongside the camper. There was no sign of Sonny Steele or the horse. She unloaded the camera equipment, took the car keys with her this time, and started, unsteadily, toward the clearing ahead. The path was uneven and the camera cases were heavy and she was beginning to get annoyed.

"Hey! I'm here!" she hollered. She moved into the clearing and looked around. "I'm alone! No troops!" She set the cases down and waited. She heard nothing. Then, suddenly, he was there, moving toward her from beneath an outcropping of trees. He was leading the horse.

"Come on," he said.

She picked up the cases and followed him. She stumbled along for a little while. Then her heel twisted and she went down. He turned.

"I think my leg's broken. What do we do? Shoot me?"

He looked at her for a moment as if he were seriously considering it. Then he picked up the cases and she got up and continued to follow him. After a while, he put the equipment down.

"Get your camera ready," he told her.

She started to grumble, then caught herself and got busy setting up the camera and tripod.

"Okay," she said, rubbing her hands together briskly. "If you'll stand over there with that range of mountains behind . . ."

"This is all right," he said curtly. He was standing in front of an utterly uninteresting landscape: a patch of tall weeds, a cluster of scraggly trees, a clear and endless sky. It could have been any place.

"It'll look much more dramatic over by . . ."

"You can tell them it was dramatic," he cut her off again. "You've got a colorful imagination."

She swung the camera toward him. "Listen, I'm cold and I'm tired. I've been traveling all night and I don't like being talked to as if I were . . ."

"And I don't like being talked about like I'm a horse thief!"

She focused in on him, and then, without his knowing it, she turned the camera on. "You stole a horse! You *are* a horse thief!" she flared back at him.

"I took this horse because they were shooting hypodermics into him! Trotting him around on a stage with a bunch of chorus girls! He's a horse. Look at him. He's a champion!"

Hallie checked the equipment. She hoped the sound was picking up right. Steele lowered his voice and continued.

"Listen, I saw this horse run," he said. "I saw him stumble and fall back and lose his stride, and then pull himself up. I saw him stretch himself out when he didn't have nothing left to give . . . but he found it somewhere." He patted the stallion. "You won, didn't you, junkie? Hell, this horse's got a heart the size of a locomotive. He's got more soul and drive and heart than most people you'll ever know."

Steele's anger returned, but it didn't sound out of control. It sounded, Hallie thought, like a righteous accompaniment to his words. It sounded, in fact, more passionate than angry.

"And they're hanging lights all over him. They'd dress him up in short pants and have him smoking a cigar if they thought it'd sell their damned junk!"

More, Hallie pleaded silently. Give 'em hell, Sonny. She prayed he wouldn't discover that the camera was on him and already running; that he wouldn't feel betrayed and blow it all for her and for himself.

"They've got him tanked on tranquilizers and Bute. His tendon's filling up. They've got him shot full of steroids. It's just for looks and it makes him sterile—so even if you wanted to breed him and pass on them great qualities, you couldn't. . . ." He paused. "To say nothing of what the horse hisself is missing. . . .

"So I took him," he said simply. "You want to put that thing on now? If you turn that little camera on, I'll try to give you a speech."

Hallie lowered her head. "Okay," she said quietly. She looked through the lens again. "Ready."

He became immediately awkward, unsure, stiff.

"Can you see me? Can they see the horse?"

"Keep going. They can see everything," she assured him.

"Ah . . . this here's Sonny Steele," he said. Then pointing: "His name is Rising Star. And he's one of the best . . . one of the great animals in the history . . . of animals."

He looked back over at her, then down at the the ground. Then, valiantly, she thought, he forced himself to face the camera again.

"I'd like to talk to you about fairness. You've

been told a lot of lies about me. None of them are true. Well, maybe I drink now and then, but even the Pope takes a drink now and then." He hesitated. "Thing is," he continued after a moment, "this horse ain't been treated fairly. They've been having him do things he's not born to do. He ought to be lazing around some field, eating good mountain grass, standing stud. . . . He ought to be putting on weight and getting old . . . like the rest of us. . . ."

Hallie became aware of a buzzing sound that grew louder, closer. She looked up. A small jet, a privately owned Lear, she guessed, was streaking past, coming in for a landing at a nearby air strip . . . probably the little field outside of St. George that she'd passed en route. She thought about the car and motorcycle escort she'd seen. She realized suddenly that she'd heard at least two sirens passing since she'd turned onto the dirt road. She scanned the horizon for a trace of smoke or a clue to anything newsworthy that might be going on in the vicinity.

For all she knew, the plane might have been crammed with marijuana and the cops about to make the biggest bust of their careers. Or the biggest bonus. Whatever. It was strictly local; she'd bet on that.

Sonny was winding down, finishing his speech.

"He's got some rights. Maybe they bought him, maybe they own him, but there's some rights you never buy . . . even from an animal. . . ."

She remembered that he'd been on TV before. She'd watched tapes of some of his appearances. Rope tricks on talk shows. It was hardly the same. She smiled encouragingly at him.

"This horse earned a better life," he said. "I want to see he gets it."

He stopped. Hallie turned off the camera. "How are you going to do that?" she asked him.

"I'll do it." He turned away, picked up a blanket, and tossed it across the horse's back.

Hallie watched him. She wanted more but decided not to push it. She began to put away the camera gear.

"Appreciate you coming. You've got stamina," he said.

Her back was to him. She glanced over her shoulder. "Family trait," she told him. He was busy with the horse. His back was to her, too.

"You'll forgive me if I'm not set up for entertaining." He didn't even bother looking at her. "I've got to tend this horse so I can get moving."

"Where?"

He didn't answer.

"Listen," she said, "I could go with you."

"No."

"I really wouldn't be any . . ."

He turned. She thought he might be smiling. His mustache didn't give much away, but his eyes looked just a little crinkly, amused. "Trouble?" he finished the sentence for her. Then he laughed.

She laughed, too. Good sport Hallie. "Well . . . let me give you my card."

"Your what?"

She dug into her tote bag. "Sometimes you think of something you forgot to say, or . . ."— she held out the card—". . . or wish you'd said." He took it awkwardly. He turned it over once or twice, then put it into his jeans pocket. "Steele? What *are* you going to do with him?"

He picked up her camera cases and began to move toward the path. "I told you."

"You didn't tell me anything!"

"Enough," he said.

She followed him reluctantly. "Why does it have to be such a big secret?!"

"So they can't stop me!"

"From doing *what*??"

"Turning him loose . . ."

"What?" She was surprised. Shocked, maybe. "Rising Star?"

He continued down the path. "Get him back to where he was, what he was. Everything he needs to know, he knows. It's in his blood . . . just half-forgot."

She was trying to catch up to him and to keep picking her way along carefully. She settled on slowing down and staying in one piece. "That's a thoroughbred racehorse!" she shouted at his back. "They're delicate as orchids! You can't . . ."

He stopped and turned to her. "Maybe it won't work. Maybe he won't make it. But it's up to him now, isn't it?" He didn't wait for an answer. He hitched up the heavy metal cases and moved briskly along the little trail.

"Where are you going to do this?"

"You have a safe trip down, Miss," he said, pointedly ignoring the question.

"Miss, my ass! Where are you going to turn him loose? Do you know?"

"I know."

"Who else knows?"

"Maybe he does," he said with a faint smile. "Interview *him*."

"You're going to screw up your whole life!"

They'd come to the car. He put down the cases.

"I'm unscrewing it, lady." He went around to the back. She tossed him the keys and he opened the trunk and started to put the equipment away.

Time was running out. "Wendell Hixson says you forget the best part of yourself . . ."

"He's a nice man, Wendell."

"Is he right?"

"No."

Stamina, she thought. You ain't seen nothing yet, Steele. She gave it a second. Then: "She says you take her breath away."

He straightened up and peered at her over the top of the trunk. The look was enough to make her still slightly tender cheek wish she hadn't said that. But the other ninety-nine percent of her was cheering: Gotcha, cowboy! Gotcha!

"That ain't hard to do," Sonny said. "She's all breath, anyway."

"She's pretty."

He stared at her for another second, then slammed the trunk shut. "Yeah, she's pretty."

"She told me that when you two first met, you used to . . ." Hallie froze, remembering . . . trying to remember.

"Damn that woman," he said.

She snapped her fingers impatiently. "Wait a second! That place . . . that canyon where you spent your honeymoon . . . there were wild mustangs! What was the name of it?? Rim Rock Canyon!"

"Damn her," he said again. "That's the main reason I left her . . . or she left me—her big mouth! Anyway, I ain't going to no Rim Rock Canyon." He started around the side of the car.

"Listen," Hallie said. He was leaving. He was going to get the horse and take off: head for the hills, climb into the camper, and give her a hand-shake and a hearty Hi-Ho, Silver, away! She was desperate now. "I got an idea. Why don't we drive to town, have a cup of coffee, talk this over. My treat."

He didn't even bother to laugh in her face. He reached into his pocket and took out a soiled envelope. "I won't be passing a mailbox. It's got a stamp on it and everything. I'd be obliged if you'd . . ."

"Sure," she said, taking the envelope. "First one I pass. . . . Well . . . I just take the road back to that broken tree?"

"Same way you came, only backward." He handed her the car keys.

"Thanks. Don't lose my card." He patted his pocket where the card was. "Right," she said. "Well . . . good luck—wherever you're going."

"Thanks."

She opened the car door. Sonny started up the path.

"You can call me anytime," she said.

He touched the brim of his hat and kept on going.

Hallie waited a full minute. Then she switched on the ignition and backed the car down the dirt road until she found a place to turn it around. At the highway, she decided against St. George. It was sixty miles back. Before she'd found the dirt road, she'd seen a marker heralding a town in the opposite direction, practically right around the bend, named Hurricane.

It turned out to be a very small town. She spotted a pay phone outside a fly-paper café and pulled the car up to the curb in front of it. A police car was approaching. From inside the phone booth, she watched it with no real interest. She waited for the operator to get New York on the line. She watched the blue and white police car go by and saw it pass another blue and white police car, and then Les Charles' voice was who-what-where-and-when-ing her over the wire.

"That's what I said, Les—I've got him on tape, talking pictures, and wait'll you hear the talk. People are going to eat him up. Now tell me an affiliate between here and Vegas so I can get this on the cable."

"Hold your horses," the WBC news director said. "I'm checking. Did you hear what I said?"

"I'm trying to convey a sense of urgency. I want this to make air today."

"KLSG-TV in St. George, Utah."

"Now pay attention; this is crucial. I need a camera crew to meet me at a place called Rim Rock Canyon. It's in Utah. Check the Auto Club or something."

"When do you need them?"

"They should start now because I don't know when I'm going to get there, and I don't know when he's going to get there. And they better be prepared to camp out because I get the feeling there's no Hilton in this place. I mean, it's a place *horses* like. And, Les? When Steele gets there, he's going to turn Rising Star loose."

"What???"

A third police car passed the phone booth. Hallie put on her tinted glasses and turned her back to the street. "Twelve million bucks' worth of thoroughbred loose in 'horse heaven.' Think it's a story?"

"Stick with the lunatic. Tape everything!"

"Won't work," she said. "He doesn't want me around."

"Nobody wants you around. That never stopped you before."

She thought about it. He was right. What was she doing taking no for an answer . . . from a *cowboy*, for Chrissakes? "Les, I'm tired. Just get the crew. I'll talk to you later." She hung up.

Outside the booth, she looked both ways along the dusty main street. There was a squad of cop cars now off to the left. And a mailbox to her right. She turned right, rummaging in her tote for Steele's letter. At the box, she held the folded, smudged envelope up to the light and tried to read it. She started to tear off a corner. "A cowboy," she mumbled. "A cruddy *cowboy!*" She put the letter into the mailbox, then walked back toward the rented car.

A man in blue jeans and a plaid shirt was leaning against the front fender, watching the police activity up the street.

"What's going on?" Hallie asked him.

"Dunno for sure. They must have spotted that breakfast cowboy."

Hallie stared at the man, then looked back at the police cars. "Shit," she muttered. The man raised an eyebrow. She checked her watch. When she looked up again, the unmarked car that had passed her on the road earlier, the car that had been preceded by two motorcycles, drove by slowly. Attached to its rear bumper was a county marshal's badge.

A group of truckers left the café. One of them, a big guy, headed for a rig nearby. Hallie opened her tote bag and took out the cassette she'd removed from the camera, the video tape of Steele and Rising Star. Clutching it, she ran down the street to the truck.

"You going to St. George?"

The trucker shifted his toothpick from one side of his mouth to the other. He eyed her speculatively. " 'Less they move the road," he said.

She handed him the cassette. "I'll make it worth your while. . . ." He seemed almost disappointed when she gave him fifty dollars.

She watched the big rig move out of town. The trucker had assured her that he knew where the station was. "KLSG-TV? Passed it a hundred times." And that it would take him less than an hour to make St. George.

She hurried back to the rental car and headed for the highway at a leisurely pace. Two miles out of the little town she accelerated. She caught Steele just as he reached the highway. She screeched onto the dirt and stopped dead ahead of him.

He slammed on the brakes, quickly checked to make sure the horse was all right, then jumped angrily out of the Tioga. Hallie was out of her car.

"Lady," he said quietly, "you're wearing out your welcome."

"You can't go into town. There's a cop convention . . ."

Sonny glanced quickly at the road, then back to her.

". . . I counted three prowl cars, two motorcycle cops, and a county marshal—all waiting for you."

He glared at her. "You told me nobody was going to follow you!"

"Nobody did! An expert got me out of that hotel."

He'd moved past her to the edge of the highway and was peering toward town. "Expert, huh?" He got into her car and moved it out of the Tioga's path. Hallie watched him. She waited. As soon as he'd stopped the car and started back to his camper, she ran for the trunk and pulled out the camera cases.

"Wait a minute!" she called, running toward him as fast as her boots and baggage allowed.

"Why? You want to film the capture?!"

"I'm in as much trouble as you are!"

"What are you talking about?"

"I can't go back there." She bent her knees so that the cases rested on the ground, but she didn't let go of the handles. "If I go back there, I'll have to tell them everything I know. *Everything!* And if I don't, they said I'll go to jail! Mis-prison of felony—that's what they call it . . . ! And that's from the legal department!"

She half-dragged, half-carried the camera cases over to the Tioga.

"Then tell them. I'll be gone by then, anyway!" He had the door to the camper open and one foot inside before he noticed her scooting around the front. She opened the other door and started shoving her equipment in. "Hey, what are you doing?"

"I can't tell them! I can't 'divulge sources' and expect anybody ever to tell me anything again." Enough with the whining and wringing of hands, she thought. Let's get this show on the road. But then she saw his face and decided she needed insurance. "And . . . I'd have to tell them about Gus. . . ."

That did it. He sat there turning purple with

only his pretty blue eyes and blond mustache clashing. Suddenly there was the whomp, whomp, whomping of a helicopter overhead. He spun to look at it and she scrambled up into the seat. He watched the helicopter, then gave her a last flash of murderous rage, then threw the camper into gear and eased out onto the highway.

They rode in silence. Sonny was grim, checking the mirrors and the progress of the helicopter, which was now heading away from them. Hallie sat huddled as far from him as possible. She wanted a cigarette—to smoke, to chew; it didn't matter—but she had him figured for a latent ecology nut, and this was no time to rattle his cage, or his closet.

He turned off the highway onto another dirt road. When he slammed on the brakes, she was jolted forward and ready to fight . . . until she saw what he'd seen. The road was washed out. A mass of rocks blocked the way. "Damn," Sonny said.

Rising Star stretched his neck and put his head down near Hallie's shoulder. "At least somebody's friendly around here," she said, patting his nose.

"He doesn't know who you are, that's all. . . . Listen, what are you planning on doing—being on the run the rest of your life?" He was backing the camper onto the highway again.

"Once you let the horse go, nobody's going to give a damn about me."

He lapsed back into silence. A sign on the highway said: HURRICANE—CITY LIMIT.

"You can't go into that town!" Hallie was aghast. "Didn't you believe me, about the cops . . . ?"

"They got helicopters in there, too?"

"Of course not. It's just this little teeny-weeny town . . ." She shut up. He was right. If there were three cop cars in Hurricane, there'd probably be battleships in St. George. There wasn't really much choice. She leaned back and scrunched down a little as they came into town behind a school bus full of kids.

The barricade was visible at the other end of the main street. A car pulling a horse trailer had been stopped. Uniformed cops talked to the driver while a small crowd of locals stood around watching. Sonny eased the Tioga toward the curb behind a parked truck.

"What're we going to do?" Hallie asked.

He was still figuring it out. Finally he said, "Get on the floor."

"What??"

"Do it! Get on the floor!"

She scrambled down. He glanced into the rearview mirror. Two motorcycle cops were leaving the small café, crossing to their parked bikes. Sonny slipped into the back of the camper and began to saddle Rising Star.

"What . . . what are we doing?" Hallie whispered.

He was working feverishly with the saddle. "*You're* going to stay right there. When I go out the back, you're going to count to sixty and . . ."

"Out the back?! Wait a second! What are you . . ."

"When you hit sixty, drive this thing the hell out of here. The cops will chase me."

"You're crazy!"

He bent to tighten the cinch. "Go to a place called Cisco Falls. There's a lake at the bottom of some dry red cliffs . . ."

"Where's Cisco Falls?"

"Find it. You found me!" He opened the back door.

"Wait a minute!" Hallie shouted. "Oh, please! There's a dozen cops out there! You'll never make it!"

"That's up to him," Sonny said, stroking the horse. "No excuses, junkie. Tendon's going down and you ain't wheezing . . . and," he said very softly, "goddamn, I've seen you run." He backed the horse out. "Start counting," he called, then slammed the door shut.

All hell broke loose before she got to ten.

Stretched nearly flat against the dazzling stallion's back, Sonny took off across the street, heading straight for the driveway of a welding yard. The motorcycle cops skidded into a turn and roared off after him.

Up the street, sirens began to scream. Red lights spun wildly. The squad cars at the head of the highway gunned their motors and backed every which way with a great screeching of tires and grinding of gears.

An old rattletrap that had swerved to avoid Sonny backed into one of the squad cars with a terrible crunch. The siren died loud and pitifully. Two other blue-and-whites careened down the street, separating at the scene of the tangle and scraping fenders on the other side. One of the cars veered off after the motorcycles. The other executed a lunatic turn and raced for the corner.

Hallie glanced hopelessly at her camera gear. Sonny and Rising Star were streaking through the yard pursued by the motorcycles and the patrol car.

". . . fifty-two, fifty-three, fifty-four . . ."

The welding yard looked like a forbidding ob-stacle course, strewn with shards of rusting metal through which a narrow path snaked. Rising Star found the path. Took it. Raced as passion-ately for the little corral at the far end of the yard as ever he had for a finish line.

The patrol car acquiesced and backed out. Hallie saw the motorcycles flounder in the soft dirt of the corral. She saw Sonny hesitate, peer quickly over his shoulder, then take the fence. Beyond was an open green field.

". . . fifty-nine . . . and sixty!" She threw the camper into gear and headed for the chaos where the roadblock had been.

How they did it, he didn't know, but halfway across the field—with the desert in sight ahead —he heard the motorcycles again, and they were gaining on him. He steered the horse toward a fringe of thicket and ducked down low as they sped through bushes and over fallen branches toward the clean stretch of sand beyond.

The motorcycles skidded wildly at the edge of the desert, but stayed on his tail. Sonny heard them and then the chugging thud of helicopter blades overhead. He urged the horse on; he urged himself. He promised them both pastures of plenty just over the next rise.

There were cop cars over the rise. And, mirac-ulously, there was water—a dam, so shallow at the far end that he could see the riverbed. He raced along the ridge of the dam with the cars in pursuit. He raced toward an oncoming motor-cycle. He guided the horse down the side of the ridge. A road ran along the bottom. There were police cars on the lower road, too. The motorcycle that descended in his wake rammed into one of them.

Then one of the cars riding the top of the ridge turned to follow him down, spun out of control, and landed on top of the car chasing him below. Hood to hood, the cars ran along the bottom of the ridge. Sonny took the horse halfway up the embankment and headed for the shallow end of the dam. The last motorcycle daredevil on his trail tore up the steep ridge, faltered, skidded, flipped over, and, finally, plummeted into the path of the strange Siamese twin below.

Sonny Steele and Rising Star splashed through the sweet, icy water at the far end of the dam, then clambered up the gentle rise on the other side.

# 12.

# WALKING

There were no falls at Cisco Falls. She had pondered that impenetrable mystery on and off for the past two hours. And, for two hours, it had remained the least distressing mystery she could ponder. It was certainly less upsetting than wondering whether Sonny Steele had been caught . . . whether Rising Star had been hurt . . . whether the trucker had delivered her film to the station manager in St. George . . . whether the meeting at Cisco Falls was a ruse on Steele's part to get her out of his dusty blond hair.

Hallie sat on the back step of the Tioga whistling tunelessly and searching the red cliffs around her for the trickle of water that might have spurred someone to christen the cold, lackluster rock farm "Cisco Falls." She whistled and searched and kept her hand firmly clamped over her wristwatch because she'd had it with checking the time. Hours. That was good enough. She'd had hours to ponder and squander and wait.

Her mind drifted back to the dangerous zone. She thought about the inordinate number of squad cars she'd passed . . . and county marshals and state troopers and motorcycle cops and circling helicopters. Her nose began to sting again, and her eyes. She swiped at them with the back of her frozen hand. Just what was she getting misty about—Steele's defeat, or her own? They seemed inextricably tied together all of a sudden.

She thought she heard a noise. She turned, trying to subdue the quick flutter of hope. "Hello?" she called softly. The red rocks were as obstinately silent as the cowboy had ever been. "Hello?" Hallie called again, loudly this time, defiantly.

Sonny Steele and Rising Star emerged from a crevice in the taciturn rocks.

"You made it!" Despite herself, she ran toward them, smiling. They both looked exhausted. The horse was nicked and bleeding, covered with dry sweat.

"There's some Witch Hazel in the cabinet over the sink," Sonny said, "and an old T-shirt by the bunk."

She hurried back to the Tioga while Sonny uncinched the saddle. He mumbled reassuringly to the horse as he worked. "I owe you one, buddy," he was saying when Hallie returned with the T-shirt and the lotion. She watched quietly as he finished unsaddling Rising Star.

It was dusk, cold and magical low in the mountains. The crisp air brought evening scents of earth and evergreens and smoky bark. The light grew pale and gray. Hallie listened to the gentle sound of Sonny's voice in the sudden stillness. She watched how lovingly he handled the horse; how gently, tenderly, he worked. After a while, she said quietly, "Nobody chased me. You were right—they all took off after you. You should have seen yourself. It was fantastic."

He looked at her a moment, took the T-shirt and the lotion, and went back to work.

"Are you surprised I got here?" Hallie asked.

"No."

She was. Surprised and proud and looking for a little recognition for her efforts. "It was on the road map," she said. She guessed he didn't know that she usually had drivers meeting her planes, taking her directly to the warmest baths in the best hotels of all the godforsaken places she visited. "I didn't have to ask anybody or anything. . . ."

He continued cleaning the horse's wounds.

"It'll be dark soon," Hallie said, rubbing her arms briskly. "How long does it take to drive to Rim Rock Canyon?"

"Couple days." He didn't look up. "But we ain't driving."

"What?"

"Cops'll be looking for that . . ."—he nodded at the Tioga—". . . everywhere. We'll have to leave it."

"And do *what*?"

"Walk." He wiped the horse down a final time and said to him, "I won't ask nothing more of you today."

For one stupid second, Hallie thought that maybe he was talking to her in that sweet and tender, grateful tone of voice. But, then, illusions were natural to people in shock. "Walk?" she muttered vaguely. He couldn't mean it.

Sears had his hands clasped behind his back. He was smiling. It was an utterly mirthless smile. It was, in fact, just a tightening of his already tense facial muscles for the sake of the hundred or so people watching the Ampco motorcycle demonstration at the convention center. Fitzgerald looked about to be sick.

"*How?*" Ampco's chairman demanded for the third time. "How could he escape? *How?*"

"Apparently he didn't know he couldn't." It was the best Fitzgerald could do. He'd tried a simple "I don't know," a shrug, a shake of his curly head.

"I see. . . . Fitzgerald?"

"Yes, sir?"

"He's not Superman. He's not invisible. He's not a . . . radically advanced thinker. He's not even well. He's . . . a cowboy. *We*—on the other hand—are, theoretically, a group of men and women who have built . . ." Sears' eyes swept the demonstration and the display areas beyond it. ". . . all this," he said. "We have money, we have airplanes, we have helicopters, we have computers. . . . How could he escape?"

"On the horse, sir."

Sears' smile faded abruptly. "Fitzgerald, find him. Find the horse. And bring them back. Use the F.B.I. Use the state police. Use helicopters. Put out a reward. A large one. Get the Boy Scouts; get the marines. Where is he, in Utah? Get the Mormon Tabernacle Choir. Have them *sing* him in, but get him!"

"Yes, sir," Fitzgerald said.

"What time is it? I'm going back to the suite . . .

to watch the news. And, for your sake, I trust there won't be a word about Steele on it."

"No, sir," the public relations officer assured him. "The operation may not have been successful, but it was discreet. No leaks. You have my word on that."

*Because they were shootin' hypodermics into him. Trottin' him around on a stage with a bunch of chorus girls! He's a horse! Look at him. He's a champion . . . !*

"You bet!" Leroy shouted. He toasted Sonny's grainy image with the bourbon, then took a slug straight from the bottle. He was sitting in the chair in front of the television set. Wendell was eating taco chips on the bed.

"He really did it this time," Wendell said mournfully. He balled up the bag of chips and tossed it onto the floor with the empty Coke cans and Leroy's socks. Then he looked at the screen again and a big grin lifted his whiskers, and the perfect teeth Sonny had bought him shone through like the sun.

*Listen, I saw this horse run. I saw him stumble and fall back and lose his stride, and then pull himself up. . . .*

Charlotta put the finishing touches on her makeup and turned back to the television set. Amen, Sonny, she thought. If that ol' racehorse done it, you can do it, too, boy. That's what you're really saying, isn't it? Well . . . She turned back to the mirror and blinked her eyes to see if the mascara was dry yet. . . . With a little luck, we'll all pull ourselves up. Even this ol' gal.

*. . . and they're hanging lights all over him. They'd dress him up in short pants and have him smokin' a cigar if they thought it'd sell their damned junk!*

Fitzgerald grimaced like someone about to be hit. He glanced quickly at the telephone on the desk in his room. It looked ominously serviceable. He considered taking the receiver off the hook. He contemplated the wording of his resignation. He slipped a Gelusil into his mouth, closed his eyes, and let Steele's words wash over him. They slapped like the last wave washing over a drowning man.

*They got him tanked on tranquilizers and Bute! His tendon's filling up. They got him shot full of steroids. It's just for looks and it makes him sterile. . . .*

Hunt Sears removed his glasses quietly and pressed his temple.

There was no television set in the Tioga. Hallie wished she knew whether the cassette had made it to the station in time—if it had gotten there at all. It had, she kept telling herself. It had to.

"Listen, I could tape a little bit along the way . . . you know, nothing that would give away where we are. Maybe I could get somebody to get it to the network like I did today. . . ." She glanced out the back door of the camper. It was pitch-black and howling out there now. Rising Star was tethered to a tree, a blanket warming his weary back. Hallie saw him in the funnel of light from the open door.

The door was ajar because Sonny was smoking things up at the stove. He was cooking chili.

Hallie moved restlessly, excitedly, from the back door to the small burners above the half-refrigerator. ". . . and since you figure it's a long trip, then that's what . . . four, five more days on the news."

He gave no indication of having heard her. He dished out two bowls of chili.

"None for me. I'm not hungry," she said. "So by the time you set Rising Star free, you'll have everybody in the country behind you."

"Then I'd just have to keep looking over my shoulder," Steele said. He sat down on one of the bunks and started breaking up crackers, tossing them into his bowl.

Hallie threw herself down opposite him. "Do you *want* to go to jail?" she asked, exasperated.

"No."

"Well, how do you think this is going to end?!"

"Not on television," he said.

Hallie stared at him, wide-eyed. For a frightening moment, she was certain that he knew about her phone call, about the reporters who would be waiting for them at Rim Rock Canyon. Impossible, she assured herself, and grabbed the bowl of chili he'd fixed for her and started gulping it down guiltily.

"Okay . . . I respect your position." She swallowed hard, coughed, tried to clear her mouth of the spicy beef while she cleared herself of suspicion. "I don't understand it. but I respect it. Lots of famous people hated publicity. I don't know how they got famous. Albert Schweitzer, Franco . . . Albert Schweitzer . . ."

He was looking at her strangely. She stopped eating. "What are you staring at?"

He just looked at her, then shook his head, got up, and went outside. Hallie rinsed her mouth with water from the canteen, then spit the red residue of chili into the sink. Then she moved to the back door. She watched Steele clucking at the horse, examining his wounds and tendon.

"I didn't mean to make you angry," she said.

He stood up. "You didn't." He stepped past her

and went back inside. He got a blanket, propped one of the bunk pillows up against the saddle, and stretched out. He put his hat over his face to shield his eyes from the light.

"What are we doing?"

"Go to sleep," he said tiredly.

"I'm not sleepy."

"You weren't hungry, either," he mumbled, half-asleep. "It's a long way."

"Where should I . . . ?"

"Wherever you want." His breathing became regular. He was asleep. Hallie watched him, troubled by her own thoughts.

She didn't remember falling asleep. He was outside, loading up the supplies when she awoke. He was strapping a blanket roll over Rising Star's saddle. Most of the food, including the coffee, was already packed.

"Hi. I'm all ready," she called to him.

"Have to get to a phone and warn Gus." He'd obviously been thinking out the day's plan. "When they find the camper, they'll trace it right to him."

She hiked up the camera cases and stepped out of the Tioga.

"What are you doing with that?"

"It's expensive equipment! I'm responsible for it. I'm certainly not going to leave it here!"

"We're walking! With our feet! There's no escalators . . . no bellhops!"

She looked over at Rising Star.

"Oh, no," Sonny said. "He's not carrying it . . ."

"I didn't ask . . ."

". . . and *I'm* not carrying it . . . and you *can't* carry it."

"The hell I can't!" Where were her arm muscles

now that she needed them? They were burning: stringy, stinging, pathetic muscles burning all the way from her long neck to her slender wrists. "I've carried this stuff plenty of times." She set the metal cases down.

"Up the escalator at Bloomingburg's?"

"Blooming*dale's*! And what do you know about New York?"

"Ever hear of the Madison Square Gardens?"

"No!"

He didn't even notice her sarcasm. "Well, they got rodeo there," he told her as if she wouldn't know. "It's a damned big thing, and I've been in it."

"I've been to the rodeo! Twice!"

"Did you stay for the rattlesnake roundup??"

"Sure! I stayed right to the end!"

"Well, they don't have one! How's anybody going to round up a rattlesnake?"

She ran her hand through her hair and stretched her aching neck. "I was just trying to be pleasant! You get yourself so worked up!"

He put a rucksack, through which she could see the outline of the enamel coffeepot, on top of the saddle and fastened it with a length of rawhide.

"What do I have to be worked up about?" he said. "I've got a stolen horse, everybody but the coast guard after me, nothing but open country to cross, and now I'm carrying a crazy woman wearing shoes from Bloomingburg's—thinks she saw a rattlesnake roundup!"

He turned to her. "Well, pick it up, if you're taking it." He started away, leading Rising Star. "'Cause it ain't going on my horse."

She took a deep breath, adjusted the tote bag and the little tape recorder hanging from her shoulder, picked up the camera equipment, and hobbled after him. "Your horse," she grumbled.

It had taken her half an hour to drive from the main road to the bottom of the cliffs yesterday. It took them several hours to trudge over the same terrain this morning. And she didn't remember the road being half so rocky or so pocked with ankle-deep trenches of stagnant water.

The bottoms of her jeans got soaked. She rolled them up but they kept making weird sloshing sounds against the soft leather of her boots as she walked. The boots themselves? Forget it! Caked with mud, they fought back by leaking and rubbing and introducing her to corns and blisters she'd never known before.

She was aching when they got to the grove of trees near the farmhouse. Most of her was aching; her arms were ready for extreme unction.

"Set that stuff down," Sonny said. She uncurled her fingers painfully and lowered the lead cases.

He had tied Rising Star to a branch, set down his own pack, and was now searching his jacket pockets for something. "Want to borrow a dime?" Hallie asked.

"Seen my glasses?"

She shook her head no.

"Must have lost them yesterday. Let me have your sunglasses."

She handed them to him. "They're prescription."

He took them, anyway. "You wait here with him. I'll be right back." He put on the glasses and stumbled off toward the farmhouse.

Hallie called after him. "Suppose you're spotted. What do I do if you don't come back?"

"Call your lawyer," he said, and tugged his hat down low.

A rock-bordered pathway led up to a tidy front porch. There was a shack out back, near the vegetable garden. Sonny knocked at the door and looked over the rims of the tinted glasses at the sweet-smelling produce coming up beside the shack.

The door opened. He pushed the glasses back up onto the bridge of his nose and strained to see through them. There was a wide man in the doorway. He appeared to have a beard—a peppery beard, darker, shorter, neater than Wendell's. He had a pleasant manner, too. His "Hello" was warmer than Sonny had expected.

"Yes, sir!" Sonny said. "Well, I was wondering if you could help me. I . . . my car broke down up the road. I got a friend over in Mesquite who's been having a little bit of trouble. He's waiting on me. I'd be obliged if I could use your phone . . . just for a second. I'd be happy to pay for it."

The farmer pushed the screen door open and pointed inside. "Yeah. We got a phone. Come on in."

"Thank you." The house was dim compared to the sunlight outside. Sonny followed the farmer's footsteps through the front room. He kept the glasses on and walked very carefully behind the man.

"Phone's in here. Help yourself."

He was uncomfortable as he dialed. He was worried about talking in front of the farmer. Sonny kept glancing over at the man while he waited for Gus to pick up. Finally, the man sensed his discomfort, quit staring at him, and stepped out to the porch.

"Gus," he said softly when the old man had answered, "it's Sonny. I don't have time to talk. Just listen to me . . . listen real careful. Some men will come to you, probably police. They'll ask you about the camper. You tell them I stole it. Say it, Gus: 'Sonny stole the camper.' No, Gus, I bought it for you, remember? And when I see you again, I'm going to buy you a nice new one. But you tell the people when they come that Sonny stole the camper. . . . Try to remember it. Got to go, friend."

He hung up and headed out of the house. The farmer was sitting on the porch railing, chewing on a cigar. Sonny reached into his pocket. "Much obliged for the use of the phone," he said, pulling out a few wrinkled dollars. "Five ought to cover it." He was smoothing and counting out the bills.

"Mr. Steele . . ." the farmer said. And Sonny froze.

"I don't want your money. I saw you and the horse on television. And . . . well, I'm proud to help you any way I can. Right now, the best thing is to get you out of this county."

He stared at the man until the icy knot of fear in his gut melted, until he could make sense of the words and fight down the new thickness in his throat. "Yes, sir," he said finally.

By late afternoon the farmer, Joseph Cloud, was driving his big stock truck to town. In the wood-slatted trailer of the truck, Rising Star rode amidst cows, sheep, a few pigs, and some squawking chickens. Hallie and Sonny lay on their stomachs in the stinking hay. She held a scarf over her nose and mouth. It was an Yves St. Laurent scarf, but the sheep who'd eaten the signature off it didn't seem very impressed.

Hallie was allergic to wool. Now she discovered that her allergy included wool on the hoof. Her eyes and nose were red, wet, and beginning to swell.

"How's life on the run suit you so far?" Sonny said.

She glared at him.

"What's the matter with your eyes? They're all puffed up, starting to look like traffic signals. . . ."

"Derrific," she said. "Very fuddy!"

Cloud rapped on the window of the cab and they lapsed into silence. The stock truck slowed, then stopped at the edge of a one-street town. A sheriff's car was parked alongside the road. The uniformed man held his hand up and Cloud leaned out the window to talk with him.

"Edwin," Cloud said, "how's the day? Treatin' you good?"

"Going by all right," the sheriff replied. "Got the whole world looking for that cowboy."

"Probably over that mountain by now. I wouldn't worry about it, Edwin. May as well cat-nap on your porch."

"Tell you the truth, wouldn't want to find him, anyway. 'Cept for that damned reward. Fifty thousand dollars—did you hear about that? That's a mound of money."

In the rear of the truck, Hallie gasped. Sonny clamped his hand over the scarf that covered her mouth, then released it. He appeared to be stunned by the news, as well.

"Well," Cloud said to the sheriff, "don't get your hopes up." He waved and continued on through town.

At dusk, the stock truck ground to a stop at the end of a dirt road at the base of the mountains.

Joseph Cloud stepped out of the cab. He stretched, moved to the rear of the truck, and unlatched the gate. He scanned the evening sky and nodded to Sonny and Hallie. When the ramp was set up, Sonny put the saddle on Rising Star and let him out. Hallie followed, sneezing and wheezing, her arms wildly overloaded.

"Excalante's just about six miles northeast," the farmer said. He went back to the cab of the truck and pulled out a duffle bag, which he handed to Sonny. "Don't know where you're headed, but . . . better have some things to hold you. There's bread and cake, coffee, and some utensils. Jar of stew. And I threw in a bottle of something to keep your blood circulating."

"Sure don't know how to thank you."

"No need," Cloud said, closing up the truck.

"Well . . . there aren't many people you'd trust fifty thousand dollars' worth."

Cloud replaced the pins and tested the rear gate. He didn't look at Sonny. "You'd better get out of here before it comes to me what I'm passing up," he said. Then he got back behind the wheel and turned the truck around expertly. He was gone as the last rays of sun moved over the foothills.

Sonny and Hallie stood in the dying light a moment longer. Then he threw the duffle bag over Rising Star and started off toward the hills. Hallie stared down the road. Only the thinnest trail of dust marked the truck's departure. She waited until the dust settled; then she picked up her equipment and set off after Steele. She was still wheezing. "Oh, my God!" she said.

She avoided her wristwatch again. Her legs and arms were giving her more information than she could handle, anyway. They told her that she'd gone far enough. Her breath, or lack of it, seconded the motion. It was dark and cold and uphill all the way now. The gently sloping foothills had long ago given way to rougher territory.

"Could we . . . rest . . . a bit?!!" She tried to infuse the words with sound, as well as wind.

"Not yet!"

"When?" she wailed. "When you're tired?"

"I *am* tired, lady!"

She bent her knees and let the cases sit on the ground a moment. If she released the handles, she knew, nothing in the world could induce her to pick them up again. "Where . . . the hell are we?"

"You're not in jail. . . . Look at it that way."

She made a face at his back, picked up the camera equipment, and put one aching foot in front of the other again. "I can't . . . go . . . any . . . farther."

"Sure you can," he insisted. But she could hear a trace of breathlessness whistling through his words. "Hell," he said, "I've seen guys go through stuff . . . you wouldn't believe. I knew a guy . . . misjudged a Brahman once . . . put a rib through his right lung . . . couldn't hardly breathe. Got right back up on the *rankest* bronc there and did his eight seconds."

"I'll never . . . understand . . ." she wheezed, ". . . why you find . . . that kind of . . . behavior . . . admirable."

"Gets you up the hill."

"I've . . . gotta . . . sit . . . down."

He kept on walking.

"Just . . . for . . . a . . . minute!?"

No answer.

"Hey, Steele!" she hollered. She took another breath. "Sonny!!" She put the cases down and cupped her hands around her mouth, and with all the strength she had left, she bellowed: *"Norman!"* Then she sat down quickly.

He stopped and turned toward her slowly. "How do you know 'Norman'?"

She tossed back her head and took a great gulp of cold mountain air. Then she let her head fall forward. "I never . . . divulge . . . sources."

He walked over to her and nodded grudgingly. Then he actually smiled. She looked up at him in the moonlight and saw him smiling. "Sure do your homework, don't you?" he said. Big white teeth grinning down at her. Crinkly eyes half-shadowed by his hat.

There were stars behind him, the whole Milky Way, but the ones making a halo around his hat reminded her of the electric horseman . . . of the majestic cowboy who had ridden down the center ramp and out the nightclub door. If she hadn't been short of spit and breath, she'd have smiled back, probably. But, as things stood, her dry lips would have stuck to her dry gums like Velcro. It seemed best to sit and wheeze awhile.

He reached down and picked up her camera case.

She stood, took two steps, tripped, cursed, and followed him.

"You know," he said when she'd caught up to him, "if you just . . . think about something else . . . it's easier. Keeps your mind off . . . your feet."

She hadn't the energy to debate survival techniques. She hadn't even the energy to nod morosely.

"You know 'The Star-Spangled Banner'?" he asked.

"What . . . ?"

"The national anthem."

"I *know* it's the national anthem . . . ! Do you mean . . . can I sing it?" She thought about it. "It's hard to sing," she concluded.

"Yeah. . . . Why is that . . . do you suppose?"

"Interesting question. . . . Maybe if we . . . just sat down . . . and discussed that . . . I was a psychology major . . . before I got . . . into journalism."

There was just the sound of their shallow breathing for a moment. Then, Sonny inhaled deeply. "Now, 'America the Beautiful,' that's an easy tune to carry."

"That's . . . a good idea . . . ! Why don't we sit down together . . . and sing 'America the Beautiful'?"

" 'Ohhhh, spacious . . . oh, beautifullll . . . for spacious skys . . . for amber waves of grain . . .' Come on," he urged. "It'll keep you going."

"Oh, God," she groaned. " 'For purple mountains . . . majesty . . . above the . . . fruited plains . . .' "

How, when, and why he decided to make camp for the night, she didn't know. She didn't care. She was . . . *more than pleased* . . . to wheeze to a halt like an old accordion collapsing in on itself. When he threw her a rumpled sleeping bag, she laid down on it. When he handed her a carrot, she chewed on it. The only decision she made or energy she exerted once he said, "Okay, this is it," was to pull off her boots before he had to cut them off.

She rested her head on a rock and, soon enough, the barnyard scents of the sleeping bag gave way to the sweet, smoky smell of the fire he built and the coffee he brewed. She watched him tethering and tending to Rising Star. She looked beyond them, above them, and saw the moon through the spiny evergreens and the stars freckling the sky.

Her eyes were half-closed when he moved back into the firelight. He poured himself a cup of coffee and sat sipping it contentedly. Her eyes were closed completely when she heard him whisper, "Hall-oween?"

She opened one eye.

"Hall-ouise?"

"Huh?" she said.

"Your name . . . Hallie. That's not your name."

Her pouty lips curled into a tired smile. "Alice," she said. "My name's Alice. My little sister used to holler for me after school. She'd yell, 'H-a-a-l-i-c-e.' So everybody started calling me Hallie."

He was leaning back against the saddle. His eyes were almost closed. "Alice Martin," he said. He nodded. "It fits you."

She closed her eyes again. "I used to bite . . . and pinch a lot, too."

"I'll bet you did."

In the distance, there was a high-pitched, almost human sound. Then another. Hallie's eyes opened wide with fright.

"Mustangs," Sonny said. "Mares. They smell the horse."

Hallie looked over at Rising Star. The stallion's head was up, his ears thrust forward. He pawed the ground. There was another far-off sound in the night. Then everything was quiet again and she began to drift off to sleep.

"Well . . . how's it feel to be wanted?"

Her eyes opened quickly.

"Like me," he continued.

"What??"

"By the police."

"Oh." Well, how was she supposed to know what he was talking about? It had been stallions and mares a second ago. Now it was cops and horse thieves. She lifted her head a little and looked across the firelight at him. His eyes were closed; his head was resting on the saddle. The coffee cup was on the ground beside him, his fingers still curled around it.

She, however, had her eyes open and her head up. She wondered if her ears were thrust forward. She lay down again quickly.

"Not much fun . . . is it?" he said. "You know what you need?"

She covered herself with the sleeping bag and held the musty quilted fabric up to her chin with two hands while she waited for him to tell her.

"Pair of proper shoes," he said.

She released her white-knuckled grip on the sleeping bag and glanced guiltily at her spike-heeled boots. Then she sighed.

"Where are we going . . . ? Are we lost?" she asked him.

"Lost . . . ? No." He shifted his weight. He let go of the coffee cup and curled up on his side. "Good night, Alice," he said.

"Good night, Norman."

She closed her eyes, but they opened. They opened like cartoon eyes, like windowshades that wouldn't stay down. Only it wasn't funny. Come to think of it, neither were the cartoons in which eyelids were lowered and then rolled back up with a whole lot of flapping. Hallie sighed. Where was fatigue when she really needed it?

She could have sworn she was sleepy a minute ago. What the hell was she doing wide awake in the wilderness . . . with a bunch of horny mares that were trying to chat up the handsome stud standing over there under the tree? God! She might as well try to get some sleep in the middle of Times Square. And the lights / . . the stars . . . shit! Or "shoot." She liked that better. That down-home stuff. Shoot, who'd turned on all those stars? You, up there, don't you know it's late? Shut off those stars, put out that moon, let me get some sleep!

She shifted. The damned sleeping bag had thinned out all of a sudden. She hadn't felt anything under it before. Now it was Princess-and-the-Pea time. Oh, great! Now she could feel every pebble . . . to say nothing of the twigs that snapped under her whenever she moved . . . or the ground that had felt like a comfy cushion a moment ago but felt like a cold, damp sponge now. A cold, damp sponge on her spine all night—just what she needed! Polio under the stars.

Across the burned-out fire she saw Sonny sleeping. His arm twitched. She wondered what he was dreaming. What sort of dream would involve a twitching arm? Maybe he was trying to shake something off. . . . Maybe he felt like something—or someone?—was dragging on him and he wanted to get rid of it . . . or them . . . or her . . .

Well, tough! Too damned bad! Did he think this was a picnic for her?! Well, brother, Central Park fulfilled her wildlife needs *totally.* Oh, God, oh, shoot, oh, shit. She couldn't sleep.

And he could. It was bad enough having insomnia alone. But there was nothing worse, nothing lower, than being awake watching somebody else sleep. And he looked so peaceful! How could he? Hadn't he scaled Everest with her today? Didn't his toes pinch just a little? Wasn't he worried about tomorrow? Tomorrow?—Hallie flinched. Tomorrow, they'd start walking again! Walk, walk, walk. She wondered which songs he'd choose for tomorrow's walk. She hoped he'd had it with the patriotic medley.

"The Bear Climbed Over the Mountain"—now, that would be perfect. *The bear climbed over the mountain . . . the bear climbed over the mountain . . . the bear climbed oh-ver the mooouuunn-ton . . . and whaddyathinkhesaw? He saw another mountain . . . he saw another mountain . . . he saw . . .*

She sat bolt upright. She looked at her watch. Then she felt around for her tote bag. It was out of reach, of course. It was near the campfire. She climbed out of the sleeping bag and crawled across the cold, hard, rock-strewn ground to it. She started rummaging through it. She found broken cigarettes and tobacco that got under her finger-nails and would stink up her whole hand . . . and she found matchbooks and a credit-card case, her wallet, her phone book . . . Ah, the pill bottle.

Or the pill *tube*. The brown plastic tube with the white plastic child-proof cap that she could never open. She shook the prescription bottle, then threw it back into her purse. No problem with child-proof caps. No problem; no pills! She reached back in and found the Bufferin bottle and shook two out. She reached for the cold coffee pan. Norman stirred.

He made a sharp sound, mid-dream, and opened his eyes. And there she was—oh, God!—leaning over him with that fury peculiar to in-somniacs who got caught on mountaintops in the middle of the night without a sleeping pill to their names. It crossed her mind that Sonny Steele was one cool cookie to wake and find her hanging there—staring down at him with her brows homicidally furrowed—and not start screaming.

"What're you doin' up?" he asked.

"Nothing much."

"You had a hard day. Just scrunch down in that sleeping bag."

She shook her head. She almost laughed; or cried. "I wish it were that easy. I don't sleep . . ."

"Never?" he said lazily. "How old are you?"

"Not . . ." she amended, "in front of someone I don't know."

"You slept last night."

"The hell I did. . . . Not in front of a stranger."

He slid up a bit, propped his head higher on the saddle. "Afraid of what you're going to look like with your mouth open?"

"You've got a mean streak."

What he had, a second later, was her wrist, and he was pulling her closer. "No," he said quietly. "No, I don't."

Her face was inches from his. Her head started to hurt from the effort of focusing. She felt like she was falling into his eyes. "I still pinch and bite," she warned.

He nodded slowly. "That's okay."


There were three limousines lined up in front of Caesar's Palace. The lead car featured a small bronze replica of Rising Star on its hood. From the spacious back seat, Hunt Sears gazed at the symbol, then turned toward the hotel entrance where a crew of night workman were taking down the "Welcome, Ampco" sign.

"They found her business card," Fitzgerald continued. He was perched uncomfortably on the jumpseat. The jumpseat was comfortable; the public relations man was not. "A bunch of rangers, I think. Oh, and state police, too. They found the camper . . . there were even horse footprints in the damned thing, in the *living room*, if you can believe that. He'd rigged up some sort of harness affair to stabilize the horse."

"Let's go." Toland signaled the chauffeur. He rapped on the thick glass partition and the lead car glided away from the curb. Toland was sitting beside Sears in the back seat. He reached for the telephone.

"If she's with Steele, then the network will know where they are," Sears said.

"Well, Mr. Sears, that's the news department. . . . I don't think they'll give us that information."

Sears didn't even look at Fitzgerald. He turned to Toland, who was talking to the company pilots, telling them they were on their way to the airport.

"Are you saying," Sears asked, "that we spend eighty to one hundred million dollars buying television time, and we can't get a simple piece of information?"

"No, no, no, no . . . I'm not saying *that*," Fitzgerald insisted.

Toland hung up the phone. "You don't ask the news department. You ask the advertising department," he instructed Fitzgerald. "*They* ask the news department."

# 13.

# TRAVELING LIGHT

She awoke very early. The mountain air was crisp and cool. The new day's sun made the damp trees glisten; made rainbows rise magically from branch to branch; shone on her sleepy face and warmed her cheeks.

She awoke very nervous. She lay very still. She lay beside him feeling his soft breath on her neck, feeling his body curved around hers with mystical precision. She lifted his hand, the one that was resting lightly on her breast, and slid out from beneath the blanket. His fingers remained gently curled. She got to her knees on the dew damp ground and stared at him.

He was sound asleep. His lips were parted, his eyes closed; his eyelashes, she noticed, looked soft as feathers. The breeze that ruffled his hair as he slept moved the tiny feathers of his lashes. She almost reached out to touch them, or to run her finger over his parted lips, remembering how unexpectedly soft they had been and warm.

She stood instead. She turned and saw the lake nearby. It was like a gift to wake up and discover a lake streaked with sunrise. It was like an extension of the night, she thought. Before he awoke, she had been for a swim in the icy water. She had dusted the earth and leaves from her clothes and rubbed the mud off her boots. She brushed her hair, swept it back from her tingling face, and brushed it until her arms ached.

When her hair was still moist but gleaming, she climbed back up the little rise that led to the camp. She stared at Steele with apprehension. He was still asleep and, suddenly, still a stranger.

She watched him a moment, looked at her camera case, then looked toward the horse. The exquisite thoroughbred was standing almost in silhouette against the crystal lake and the mountains beyond. Like an addict, Hallie couldn't resist. She opened the metal case and started to hook up the camera. Rising Star whinnied. Sonny Steele woke up. Hallie quickly put the equipment away.

"Morning . . . I'm still here." She laughed a short, nervous laugh. "There's some coffee from last night . . . might be cold."

He stared at her as if she were from Mars. Finally, he said, "Probably is, if you didn't heat it."

"And some cheese . . ."

"Cheese!" He shuddered at the thought, got out of the blankets like an arthritic cricket, dragged himself over to the horse, and started checking Rising Star's tendon.

"You're all bent," Hallie said. "Are you sick?"

"No. Just bent."

"Have some cheese," she urged. "They say that breakfast is the most important meal of the day."

"I'm the one that said it."

"Are you sure you're not hurt?"

"Parts of me wake up faster than other parts," he explained. "Broken parts take longer."

He moved stiffly to the campfire and put his hands out in front of him, feeling for the non-existent warmth. It occurred to her that she might have rekindled the fire. He was working on it now. His silence bothered her. She filled it with nervous nonsense.

"I would have gotten a cab . . . left you a little note . . . you know, 'Call me,' with my telephone number . . . my answering service number, actually . . ."

"Hey," he said as she trailed off, "what's bothering you?" He moved to her, smiling. "It was just you and me last night. . . ." She looked down at her boots. There was fresh mud on one of them. "It's not going to be on television . . . is it?"

"I don't know what you're talking about!" Her voice went up an octave somewhere in the middle of the sentence. She had snapped back too quickly, too guiltily, she knew. "The trouble is," she began to explain in the same mindless, unhappy way, "you get up slowly and I get up fast. It's the way I was brought up; we got up and we got to work."

"Hell, I grew up getting up. I was up before you had the sun in your room."

"Okay, you get the getting-up medal. Are we in a hurry? I thought we were supposed to be in a hurry."

He smiled at her and lifted his coffee cup in a toast. "Morning, Alice," he said.

Exasperated, she began to fold up the sleeping bag.

"You're right," he said. "We're running late. How about we lighten up a little?"

Her back was to him as she brushed a compost of twigs and dirt from the bottom of the bag. "Well, it *would* help." She was all business now. "We're going to be traveling together for . . ." She heard the noise and turned, horrified, to see Sonny tossing the camera case over a ledge. He calmly tossed the second case after it.

"There," he said, all white teeth and crinkly eyes again. "All lightened up."

By mid-morning she had almost adjusted to the fact that the camera was unalterably gone. She tried not to think about it—which was no easy thing considering how awesomely beautiful the landscape through which they traveled had become. She kept framing shots in her mind, feeling a quick stab of loss, then finding another vista to focus on. It was not merely mountain after mountain, but range beyond range that stretched before them under a clear, cold sky.

It helped to remind herself, every time the itch to record their journey crept up on her, that she was a reporter, not a photographer. She began to report, to create a narrative in her mind, describing what she saw and how it felt. Sometimes, she didn't understand what she felt, and sometimes she didn't know what she saw.

A bird soared, swooped, above them from one mountain crag to another. "It's an eagle," Hallie said.

"Hawk."

"If we pass an eagle, let me know."

The walking was much easier without the equipment. That bothered her for a while. Then her feet made up for the loss.

Sonny began to work with Rising Star. Hallie watched, fascinated as the cowboy introduced the stallion to new experiences, new skills he'd need to survive in the wilderness.

When they came to a steep embankment, the horse shied away from the ledge nervously. Hallie, working with newly acquired skills herself, made her way gingerly to the bottom. Sonny tightened the cinches on Rising Star's saddle and climbed atop the horse. With great patience and murmured encouragement, he forced the horse to slowly walk down the slope, then up again. After a while, Hallie noticed that they were making a circle, Sonny and the horse—they were moving up and down the embankment in a circle.

"Why doesn't he just walk down the hill?"

"He thinks the whole world's a riding ring or a racetrack."

"What do you do about that?"

"Practice," Sonny said.

The sun seemed to her to be setting awfully early. She shivered and looked at her watch. It was only noon. The sky was lead-gray. She was freezing. He took a blanket from the saddle and wrapped it around her.

"How cold does it get in New York City?" he asked.

"Cold, but nothing like this."

He laughed. "Yeah? Well, this ain't nothing. This here's springtime compared to some places. . . ."

"I've been to Alaska, you know. It wasn't as cold as I thought it would be. . . ."

"Well, see that."

"I wasn't wearing a denim jacket in Alaska!"

A light snow had begun to fall. They moved through it. Hallie pulled the blanket over her hair and lowered her head. The wind had been tearing at her face. Her cheeks felt raw and her eyes stung. She walked with her head down, following Sonny's footprints in the snow.

"You look like an Indian," he said.

"Big deal. You look like a cowboy."

The snow let up. A bright sky and towering cliffs loomed in the distance.

"You know, I didn't see any falls at Cisco Falls," she told him.

"Ain't any. Hell, you can name anything anything."

They followed a stream to the base of a high ridge. Hallie sat under a tree while Sonny continued to work with the horse. Rising Star was still having difficulty with steep paths, and the stallion appeared to be skittish around water, too. Hallie took off her boots and rubbed her feet while Sonny marched the horse up and down an embankment, working him closer to the edge of the stream each time.

". . . It's the same stuff you drink," she heard him telling the horse. "Ain't half-bad back of bourbon, neither . . . but it can be walked in and swum across, too. . . . If you don't get to know that, junkie, you ain't gonna make it."

He rode the horse up the embankment toward her. "You ever try to see the sea from the Sea-Vista Hotel in Needles? There ain't even a bird-bath for three hundred miles."

She laughed.

" 'Mountain-View' hotel's always downtown Kansas. Like them people see all that stuff in the stars at night—guys riding in chariots . . . and see bulls, snakes, and chickens and shit. . . . What's this guy's name, 'Rion' . . . ?"

"Orion!"

" 'Orion'—he supposed to have a belt? I never seen no belt up there. You ever see a belt? Tell the truth."

She shook her head. "No . . . 'I never seen no belt.' "

"Well, there you are. . . . Sometimes, when it's real clear, though, I still take a look." He got down from the horse, took the reins, and led him toward the stream, circling, talking.

"Probably there was a falls here once. This whole area was underwater millions of years ago. You look real close . . . take your time . . . you can find skeletons and weird-looking fishes in the hard pan . . . long gone. . . . All these mountains, everywhere you can see, were under an ocean. . . ." He stopped and looked up to where she was sitting. "What are you laughing at?"

"Nothing. I was just enjoying the fact that you know all that. It's interesting."

"This country is where I live. You know where the subways go, don't you?"

"Not lately!"

He led Rising Star back up the bank and tethered him to a tree near the one Hallie was leaning against. "Yeah, you do!" he said. "How'd you know how to find me? There must have been seventy, eighty reporters in that hotel room. You're the one that found me!"

"I had a hunch or two and a head start."

He picked up her boots and examined them with dismay. "No," he said, handing them to her. "You had more than that. . . . You're good, lady. Come on, Alice, time to go." He grabbed his bag and helped her up.

By the time she eased her aching feet back into the boots, he'd brought Rising Star into position in front of her. He made a stirrup with his hand and motioned for her to get up on the horse.

"Put your foot up here."

"What . . . ?? But I . . . I don't know how to ride."

"You aren't going to ride. You're just going to sit on him."

"Listen, I'm not interested in horses! They're too . . . big!"

Sonny shook his head sadly. Then he sighed. "There's not a mean bone in his body," he said as if she'd broken his heart. "Now, come on, we can't make any time with you in them spiky shoes. . . . Come here. Stick your foot in here."

She put her foot in his hand and he helped her onto the horse. She held onto the saddle horn with two hands.

"Should I p-p-pet him?" she asked as Sonny led the horse.

"Do what you want . . . he ain't no dog!!"

Things began to look different from her new height. They were moving steadily up the mountain, but it seemed as if they were traveling from one world to another. Cloud mists spread like curtains in their path. A wind would part the curtains and, though they had been passing through a green valley a moment before, the earth might suddenly be bare; where the ground had rolled gently, craggy hills and sheer cliffs would appear unexpectedly. On the other side of a boulder or through a mountain pass, a rushing stream would feed the roots of wind-twisted trees and clumps of wildflowers sprouted from stones. Arid earth gave way to rich brown or sometimes astonishingly green land. The valleys lay in rainbow patches all around them. Snow-covered peaks reached toward the endless sky.

They made camp for a while. Sonny continued Rising Star's lessons and checked his tendon and healing wounds. Hallie stretched out on a sun-warmed rock some distance from them. She lost track of time. She sat up abruptly and searched in her bag for some paper. She found a few sheets at the back of her phone book and tore them out and began to write.

Later, when Sonny approached, she whipped the pages behind her back. "Oh, no, you don't . . ."

"What've you been doing?

"Oh, no, please," she said plaintively, "you're not going to throw these away, are you? They're just notes."

"Notes . . . ? Let's see them."

She showed them to him reluctantly. "They're just notes," she promised as he looked over the pages.

He handed them back to her and shrugged. "Looks like Russian."

"It's my handwriting."

"Read it.'

"No . . . I . . ."

He cocked his head and studied her. "Secrets?" he asked.

"Oh, for goodness . . ." She reassembled the pages and began to read in a flat, perfunctory way: "Something new is happening to me—more precisely, to my eyes. I feel I'm seeing this country as if for the first time . . . not looking down from a jet thirty thousand feet above, but from the low angle of a . . ." She hesitated, then continued in a softer, more natural tone: ". . . of a man who means to cross it on foot . . . leading a thoroughbred stallion to a secret destination, to a private goal . . ."

She looked directly at Sonny now. "To a 'fairness' he hopes to find in these valleys, valleys that are marked and lined like the man himself." She lowered her eyes suddenly. "I can't. It's just for me. Just my notes . . ."

He was watching her, waiting. She continued. "I can turn slowly and see . . . all horizon. In every direction, a continuous meeting of sky and earth. I feel small. It's like being at sea within the vastness of America." She finished and turned to him. She was embarrassed, but she held his gaze.

He bent down and kissed her forehead. "That's nice about the mountains and the valleys."

"Nothing . . . hype," she said.

"Fooled me."

"We going?"

He moved the horse into position for her to mount. She shoved the papers into her pocket. "No, I think I'd like to walk," she said, "like you."

The wind was fierce on top of the mountain. They stood on the high plateau and looked out over a breathtaking panorama. Hallie's hair whipped wildly around her face. She lowered the blanket to her shoulders and laughed into the icy wind.

"It's like being at the top of the world!" she shouted.

Sonny laughed and moved closer to her. She opened the blanket and put an end of it over his shoulder. They stood with their arms around one another, each holding a side of the blanket. They stood for a moment in the warm tent they'd made for one another at the top of the world.

It was slow coming down, but it became apparent that Rising Star had learned his lessons. He began to travel the rocky hill with something approaching expertise. When he reached the bottom of the steep embankment, Hallie was almost as proud as Sonny.

The treacherous footpath and crags gave way to softer hills as they descended. They moved through a tangle of wildflowers toward a ridgeline. Hallie lagged behind to gather a bouquet. She had no idea what she'd do with the flowers, but as she walked she began to weave the stems together to braid them. By the time she caught up with Sonny and Rising Star, she'd decided that she was making a crown for the stallion. A graduation cap.

She hurried to the edge of the ridge and found Sonny staring down, looking perplexed. A two-lane highway, the first sight of civilization they'd encountered since yesterday, ribboned incongruously just below the ridge. On the far side of the road was a little gas station.

"That's not supposed to be there," he said. "Or we're not supposed to be here."

Hallie was incredulous. *"You're* lost?"

"About a mile's worth, looks like. Better get off this ridge."

They moved from the ridge to a steep embankment several yards away. Sonny led the horse down carefully. Hallie started to follow them, caught her heel, and tumbled suddenly. She reached out for something to grasp. There was nothing. The rocks slid out from beneath her and she rolled down all the way to the bottom.

She was scraped and dazed. Her shoulder hurt and her arm and elbow . . . and, most of all, her butt. It crossed her disoriented mind that she would never ride again. Only the absurdity of the thought brought relief. She tried to get to her feet, and, suddenly, Sonny was there.

"You all right?" He looked genuinely concerned.

"Tip-top, thanks."

But her attempt to rise made her wince with pain.

"You sure?"

"Really . . . really, let's go."

"You better sit down," he decided.

She rubbed her aching and, she suspected, splintered butt. "You don't seem to understand the problem."

"Well, lay down or something."

"And listen to you bitch about my boots? Not on your life." She hauled herself up and started to hobble gamely.

"We're making damned good time," he said irritably. "Now, relax!"

She stretched out on her side and propped her head up on her elbow while Sonny dug for something in the bag the farmer had given them. He pulled out a Mason jar of bourbon and brought it to her. She took a sip. Then he took back the jar and had a long drink.

"Something to make you feel better. We used

to call it the hair of the dog," he said, screwing on the lid.

"Hey! Don't put it away!"

He frowned at her, then handed over the jar. "You rest. I'm going to find us a place to cross that road," he said. "You okay?"

She took another sip of bourbon and nodded.

"I won't be long."

She watched him walk away. He had a very distinctive walk, she decided. Probably all those broncs and bulls he'd ridden had reshaped his bones. She thought his walk was very rugged, very masculine, very John Wayne, she decided. She liked the way he swayed and swiveled. She was acting like a goon, she decided, and then she decided to have another hit of bourbon.

Fitzgerald heard the program on his car radio on the way to work. It was one of those phone-in shows and he'd missed the beginning of it. Now the announcer said, "Doyle Hicks, go ahead, you're on the air."

"Yes . . ." the raspy voice said. "Is this Doyle?"

"Yes. Turn down your radio."

"Yes, well, I just want to say that what Sonny Steele done is wonderful news for the animals of this country! That's all I have. . . ."

A crackpot, Fitzgerald thought. A pervert's voice if ever I heard one. Must smoke three packs a day.

The next caller sounded more sensible, sounded like a concerned young woman who . . .

". . . don't see what's wrong," she was saying, "if somebody is poisoning an animal that a person shouldn't try and stop it if he can. . . ."

A radical! Probably some college kid who idolized Jane Fonda.

". . . done the same—BLEEP—thing myself if I'd had the chance. . . ." This time the voice belonged to a cowboy, a cracker, a hick—no doubt about it. "Them—BLEEP—Ampco people got no right to . . ."

Fitzgerald turned off his radio. Ampco Bleeps, huh? Who did these outraged citizens think Ampco people were? He was Ampco. He was a regular guy. A professional, a provider, a husband, and a father. Damn, Fitzgerald remembered. His son had asked him to bring home a Sonny Steele T-shirt yesterday and he'd forgotten. Where the hell was he supposed to get a Sonny Steele T-shirt? His son said that all the kids had them.

He pulled into the parking lot behind the Ampco Tower.

Upstairs, in the big conference room, Dietrich, Toland, and Sears were studying a map of Utah.

"Talk about boondocks." Dietrich tapped the map with his silver pencil.

Sears punched the intercom on the marble table. "No calls, Cynthia."

"She ordered a camera crew to meet her at Rim Rock Canyon. I suppose to photograph the, uh . . ." Toland liked to be precise.

"Ceremony," Sears helped him. "The sales figures again. Exactly."

Toland rifled through his notes. "For three days since he took the horse, office equipment has been, as predicted . . ."

"Cereal!"

"Cumulatively up thirty percent. By closing time in the east, they'd emptied the shelves." He paused to glance at the door. Fitzgerald entered.

"Yes?" Sears said impatiently. "What is it, Fitzgerald?"

"Well, sir, there is something I think you should be aware of." Fitzgerald opened the T-shirt and held it up for Sears' inspection. The center of the shirt was emblazoned with Sonny Steele's smiling face.

"Where did you get that?"

"Some kids were selling them in the parking lot, sir."

Hallie looked up and down the road. There was no sign of Sonny. That clinched it. She limped cautiously across the blacktop, then peered through the front window of the little gas station.

There was no one in the place—which turned out to be a sort of candy and souvenir shop, as well as a gas station—except a little girl who was leaning on the counter near the cash register, and looking very bored. Hallie put on her dark glasses and went inside.

"Hi," she said to the child. "What's your name?"

"Louise," the girl said. Her bored expression didn't change.

"Same as mine. You run this place yourself?"

"Your name really Louise?" she asked suspiciously.

"You bet. Your mom or dad around?"

"My mom went to get Butane," Louise said. "We're out."

"Do you have a telephone?"

"Out, too." Her elbows were on the counter. She shifted her chin from one hand to the other. "Every time it snows up at Marysville, first thing, the phone goes out. Where's your car?"

"Well, I'm sort of camping out and the car's on the blink and I wanted to let my boss know, and, uh . . . will you be going anywhere near a phone? I mean, later, like when you close up?"

"We got a phone at home."

Hallie glanced over her shoulder at the road outside. "I'll bet you could make a call for me," she said, facing the child again. "And deliver the message . . . What do you charge to make a call?"

"One dollar," the kid said without blinking.

"It's a deal." She took a pen and paper from her bag and began writing. "Will you do it? Here's the number . . . and you ask for Mr. Les Charles, and you don't talk to anybody else, and when you get him on the phone, you tell him that you're calling for me. . . ."

"For Louise."

"No . . . Yes, for Louise in Utah."

"I know what state it is."

"And when you get him on the phone . . . you tell him that Louise says to please call off the crew, and to, oh, to call off everything and that I'll explain when I see him."

A pickup truck pulled up outside. Hallie whirled around.

"I better tell him how your car's broken down," Louise said.

Two men, from a road crew by the looks of it, got out of the truck and started toward the door.

"No!" Hallie told the girl. "Never mind the car. Just the other part."

"About the flu?"

"No, the *crew!*"

The road workers came into the shop.

"I have an idea," Hallie said quickly. "I'll write out the whole message and then you can just read it to him." She ducked her head down and began to scrawl frantically.

"Her car broke down," the little girl told the men.

"Where's that, Miss?"

"It didn't actually break down. It's just the way it acts." She glanced up, smiled briefly, and lowered her head again.

"I have to call her boss from home 'cause the phone's out here."

"We could give you a lift into . . ."

"No, no, thank you . . ."

". . . or make that call for you?"

"You know, Louise, this is all too complicated," Hallie said, crumpling the paper. "I think we should just forget it. . . . Uh, I'll just grab a few staples . . ." She grabbed a souvenir ashtray and a rubber spider, slapped down a five-dollar bill, and rushed out the door. She limped and hopped back across the highway.

The Mason jar was lying where she'd left it, around the bend in the road. She looked around. Then up at the ridge. Sonny waved and started down toward her.

"It's okay. I can make it," she called.

He waited and watched her from the ridge.

"Found us a spot. How are you doing?"

"Good as new," Hallie said. "They've got a really terrific bathroom . . ."

He took the nearly empty Mason jar from her. "Serves you right," he said.

Rising Star was saddled and ready a few feet away. Sonny put the jar back in the rucksack and put the bag on the horse.

"There's a place we can cross about a mile south. Got to honk on it, though. Want to get there 'fore dark."

"We're that close?!" Panic clouded her features.

"To where we can spend the night. Inside, for a change. There's an old deserted Brand Inspectors building along the Magdalena. I hope it's still standing!"

"Isn't there some closer place . . . ?" She was worried, trying to stall. She didn't even notice that he had the horse ready and was waiting to help her mount. "I mean some closer place where you guys take horses . . . to let them go?"

"No . . . I usually use the one myself," he said.

She moved toward the saddled stallion. "You know, this place is so pretty. If I were Rising Star, I'd be perfectly happy to . . ." She sighed and got up on the horse.

"Well, you're not. Alice, do me a favor, don't go trying to think like a horse. . . . You just take the notes. I'll handle him."

She saw him smiling at her. "What?" she asked nervously.

"Don't stop worrying," he said. "You're kind of pretty when you worry."

# 14.

# PASTURES OF PLENTY

The Ampco jet touched down at the small airstrip in Utah and roared past the group of cameramen, sound engineers, reporters, and other news and network personnel assembled in front of Fitzgerald. The public relations officer waited until the noise of the Lear subsided. Then he continued his briefing.

"Although one network or reporter may think he or she deserves a monopoly on the news, we at Ampco believe that the public's right to know supercedes every other consideration. That's why we've called you here. It's good citizenship and good business."

"Where exactly are we going?" one of the reporters asked.

Fitzgerald adjusted the brim of the big cowboy hat he was wearing and turned up the fur collar on his blanket-plaid Western-style jacket. The wind was bitter. He was amazed at how easily it went right through the brand-new Levi's he wore. The jeans were so new and rigid that he could hardly bend his knees in them, but the wind wasn't having any trouble whooshing through the tight weave of the fabric. Why in the world had Steele chosen a place like this? Was he going to set the horse free, or set him adrift on an ice floe?

"If you'll just be patient and follow our instructions," he told the reporter. He saw Dietrich hurry across the field from the jet to the waiting limo, where Sears and Toland sat in heated comfort. Probably the police cars flanking the limousine were heated, too.

If only Dietrich had let him wear his own soft leather boots instead of insisting on these pointy-toed "authentic" cowboy boots. Fitzgerald looked down at his feet. How could anyone in his right mind find such shoes comfortable? He could not believe that any normal human being had naturally cone-shaped feet or toes that extended triangularly.

Sonny's boots sat next to Hallie's near the fireplace. The cabin, which had looked decrepit in the dusk, was quite cozy now. The fire had warmed the little room and bathed it in soft, dancing light. It seemed to have dried the damp mustiness from the walls and unloosed a sweet woodsy fragrance

Sonny was in an expansive, energetic mood. "Ol' Clark had this place built his first successful year of announcing," he was telling Hallie. He sat with his head propped against the mattress that doubled as a sofa; his legs were stretched toward the fire. "Had this voice like runny molasses. Sounded really great over the P.A. 'Sorry you lost, Sonny,' he'd say. . . ."

Hallie was quietly subdued, watching him. There was nothing more she could do, she kept telling herself. She'd tried to contact Les and failed. She'd tried to talk Sonny into setting Rising Star free at two different places along the way. There was nothing more she could do. She listened to him imitating the rodeo announcer's voice.

" 'Glad you came and sorry you had that tough luck.' I hadn't made a dime that year, and ol' Clark Wembly made me feel fine enough to keep trying. All those riders . . . they kept me solid. Kept me charactered . . ."

She was on top of the narrow bunk sitting on the blanket Sonny had spread over the musty old mattress. She could see his profile in the firelight. His face was lined and leathery. His jaw rippled as he spoke; his thick mustache moved. His hair was sun-streaked, golden with silver and ice-white strands threading through it. She wanted to touch his hair, but she didn't . . . not out of sudden shyness or coyness, but because she felt she didn't deserve to.

". . . ol' Wendell in his day, Woody Vinita and Dance McCue and the Lewis Brothers. You'd have loved Tommy Lewis. Took me four years to beat him. Had this stallion out of a big bay mare named 'Toots.' What a horse. Boy, am I running off at the mouth. . . ." He turned to look at her.

"I enjoyed it." She tried to smile. "When do

we get there?" she asked, letting fatigue win out over her effort.

"About midday. It's been a long haul." He got to his feet. "You held up good. You wore well."

"Thanks."

"Something bothering you?"

"What happens to you after?"

"Going to start the questions again?"

"What happens when he's loose and chasing mares? Do you just . . . do the same?"

"I don't know." He walked to the hearth and started poking at the fire. "What do you think should happen?" he asked her. "You're a clever lady. You've been taking the notes."

"You say it like it's a bad word, 'clever . . .'" She got up and joined him.

"Not 'bad,' exactly. I like that you're smart . . . but sometimes you get so busy being clever that . . . well, when was the last time you were surprised?"

"You," she said very quietly. "You were a surprise, Sonny." They stood close and silent for a moment. "I told them," she said without looking at him.

"What?"

"I called the network and told them you were going to Rim Rock Canyon. I told them to meet me there with a camera crew."

"Oh," he said softly. Then he slowly shook his head. "Oh."

"That's not all."

"Now for the bad news, huh?"

"I . . . lied to you about my going to jail. I wasn't in any trouble."

"Well, well . . ." He put the rusted old poker back up against the pile of wood they'd gathered.

"Well, well . . . what *do* you know." He looked at her a moment, then stuck his hands in his pockets and watched the fire.

"Oh, Sonny. Please don't. Don't do that! Yell at me or slap me or something!"

"Already slapped you, Alice—first time we were alone together."

"Sonny . . . I swear to God . . . I wouldn't have done it now."

"Why, you a new person?"

"I . . . it was three days ago."

He stared at her. "Yeah, a lot can happen in three days."

"I never wanted to ruin anything for you, Sonny. I had a job to do . . . I wanted a story."

"Okay. You did it! You got it!" He started to pace. "It's going to be a hell of a finish! Where's that letter I wrote to Wendell? You mail it, or is that going on TV, too? Naw, that's not news, is it? Just saying I done it and apologizing for what trouble it might o' caused him . . . that just ain't big news. No story there."

"Oh, please . . ."

He walked to where the sleeping bag was and began to unroll it. Hallie watched him in silence. Then she asked, "What are you going to do?"

"What I said."

"Why can't you just take him to *another* place and let him . . ."

He whirled to face her. "No! I want him at *this* place! Everybody done their thing, right? You did what you had to do. Ampco done what they had to do. Okay, now I'm going to do what I've got to do!"

"But you can't! They'll be there! And maybe the police!"

"I'm not going to run forever! Hell, we're all going to heaven or we're not! Besides . . . you wanted to see the finish, didn't you?"

"But not like . . ."

"Then be still," he said gently. "Be still and let it finish."

"I don't want you to be hurt."

"I been hurt and I still get up." He smoothed an edge of the sleeping bag, then stood. "But thanks for the worry."

There were tears in her eyes when she looked at him. She shook her head hopelessly. He moved to her. "Do me a favor tomorrow?" he asked. "Don't take notes."

Hallie leaned her head on his shoulder. They stood like that, not touching, just her head on his shoulder. "Oh, Sonny," she whispered into the warmth of his neck, "I'm so sorry."

He lifted her chin and stared down into her sad green eyes. He brushed his calloused hands against her cheeks, very lightly, softly; he moved his strong fingers to the velvet hollows beneath her eyes and let her warm tears wash over them.

"So sorry, so very, very sorry." She shook her head, then laid it against his flannel shirt, which smelled like the fire, smelled like burned pine, smelled like huddling together in a sleeping bag while mustangs called to each other in the windy night.

"Come on," he said. He lifted her effortlessly. He rocked her, carried her. He set her softly down on the quilted bag on the floor. "Let it finish," he whispered. His warm lips were on her cheeks. "Be still now and let it finish."

Her shoulders were shaking. He held her very close to him until they stopped. The hands that held her shoulders firmly moved across her back, traced her spine, rocked her, rocked her gently. She lay beside him on the sleeping bag in front of the fire. She held on to him although she didn't have to. Her arms reached across his broad back and shoulders, her fingers stretched to catch, to caress the unruly hair that curled down his neck. The muscles on his neck were thick and knotted. His hair was thick and smelled like the forest. She hid in it while he rocked her. She moved to the rhythm of his sounds, of his sweet, deep sighs.

It seemed to her that they did not sleep at all. It seemed to her that it was important not to. She sat facing him, leaning her moist forehead against his. He closed his eyes and she ran her fingers over his face. It seemed to her that she spent hours memorizing the hollows and hills of his face, the hard and soft places, brushing his hair back from his forehead. His forehead was wet like hers. The roots of his hair were damp. She kissed his forehead and tasted the salt of his sweat.

The fire died. Suddenly, it was dawn. An icy dawn, gray, then pink against the frost-shattered windows. Sonny wrapped a blanket around her back and held the edges together under her chin. Then he kissed her one more time. It was good morning; good-bye. It was important and bruising. She tasted the salt even when he left her to re-kindle the fire. She smelled his sweat, his warm flannel smell; she smelled the forest.

He got the fire started again, then went outside to check on Rising Star. Hallie was still sitting on the sleeping bag, wrapped in the blanket, when he returned. "Time to get going, Alice," he said.

She nodded her head. "How's the champion this morning?"

"I was going to ask you."

She smiled and got up.

By noon they'd come to a wide green meadow nurtured by an icy stream. Trees and wildflowers tufted the nearby hills. Mountains reared suddenly, majestically, beyond them. She couldn't imagine a better place in the world for Rising Star.

"Are we almost there?" she called to Sonny. He stopped the horse and looked around. He breathed in deeply. His face, she noticed, was clear and open. He looked peaceful, utterly at ease. He looked happy. Her own face felt drawn with dread.

"Better get off now," he said, reaching to help her down.

She took her feet out of the stirrups and slid into his arms. "When do we get there?"

"We are there," he said.

She looked around frantically. She heard the mustangs. They sounded very far off. They were somewhere beyond the gentle hills. Rising Star heard them, too, and danced nervously.

"But . . . wait a minute," she said. "The camera crew—they're not here!"

Sonny unfastened the saddle. "Appears not," he said to Hallie. Then he asked, "Well, Star, what do you think of the place?" He put down the saddle and began to take the horseshoes off the stallion.

Hallie turned slowly and searched the horizon. They were in a canyon, she realized. Mountains rose on every side. She had not noticed as they rode in. They had come through a pass indistinguishable from any other—a clearing between rocky cliffs. On the other side was the meadow; this grassy plain.

She looked back at the mouth of the canyon now. "They must be at another entrance," she said.

"Ain't no other entrance."

"Then hurry!" She could hardly believe their luck. Her heart began to race. "They're late, or they got lost!"

Sonny tossed one of the iron shoes into the stream. It hit a rock, skipped above the water once, then sank. The noise of metal on stone echoed loudly between the cliffs. The distant whinnying of wild horses responded eerily. Rising Star grew skittish. Sonny soothed him, clucked at him, and stroked his lustrous neck. "I doubt it," he said.

"What?"

"They ain't lost."

"Well, where the hell are they?"

He was prying another horseshoe loose. "Probably at Rim Rock Canyon," he said, without looking up at Hallie. "That's where you told them to go, ain't it? It's about ninety miles north of here."

She was still scanning the horizon nervously. She turned slowly, looking for another pass, another opening between the rocks through which a camera crew might emerge at any moment. She was ready to search the sky for helicopters and parachutes when what he said finally got through to her. Her jaw dropped and she whirled toward him.

"You mean this isn't . . . ???"

He tossed a second shoe toward the stream.

"This here's Silver Reef," he said, straightening, running his arm across his brow. "Pretty, isn't it?"

She stared at him a moment. Her eyes were wide, incredulous. "Why, you lying . . ." Before she knew what she was doing, she had run up to him and begun pounding on his chest with her fists. "You . . . you . . . !!" she sputtered wildly, breathlessly. She beat on him and he just looked at her. He didn't even try to stop her. And, finally, she laughed. She pounded on him and laughed.

"I never told you I was going to no Rim Rock Canyon," he said. "Hell, it's buried in snow."

"Where the hell are we, the Donner Pass, for God's sake?!" Bernie asked Chris. The WBC crew, bundled against the lashing Arctic winds, looked down from their platform to the caravan of desolate newcomers plowing through the knee-deep snow that filled the canyon.

"Positively surreal," Chris murmured as three big Winnebagos pulled up beside the WBC mobile unit in which he and Bernie had spent the night. Behind the rival networks' trailers, two squad cars and a big black limousine inched along. A catering truck had stopped several yards back, and plumes of smoke began to drift from its roof.

The WBC crew waved and jeered. "Some exclusive," Bernie said. But he was laughing.

Two men, one in Western gear, the other in an elegant fur jacket, were trying to hang a huge banner between two telephone poles in the snow. The banner read: WELCOME, SONNY STEELE! GOOD LUCK, RISING STAR! It whipped wildly between the men. Four uniformed police officers hurried from the squad cars to lend a hand. The first thing

they did was tackle and secure the man in the
elegant fur jacket, who was bent almost U-
shaped against the wind. Then they went after
the banner, which was flapping dangerously
between the towering wooden poles.

Dazed-looking journalists and cameramen
rushed from the Winnebagos and from a number
of Jeeps and station wagons that had stopped
on the road. Crews began to set up camera plat-
forms near the power lines. Huge spools of cable
cut wagon-wheel-like paths in the snow and thick
black ropes snaked from the spools to the poles
and back toward the trailers.

Fitzgerald, having left the banner to a select
force of police and Ampco crewmen, helped
Dietrich part of the way back to the limousine.
Dietrich's jacket was torn and soaked. He looked
like a mythical creature, an enraged, sodden
beast—half-frozen man, half-matted animal—
spewing icy smoke signals as he slouched toward
the mud-caked black car.

Fitzgerald, shivering through his blanket-plaid,
imitation Western-styled jacket, his face mottled
a matching red and blue with the cold, left him a
few feet from the limousine and hurried to the
group of disgruntled reporters who, having prepared their equipment, now waited for history to
unfold before their tearing eyes. They milled
near the catering truck demanding food, hot
coffee, and an explanation.

Toland, grim, steely eyed, with a lap robe over
his fastidious gray chesterfield, helped Dietrich
into the limousine, then got out himself to watch
Fitzgerald handle the press.

"No . . . I didn't say that!" Fitzgerald was shouting over a bullhorn one of the cops had given to

him. The fierce wind precluded his being heard any other way. His amplified voice echoed piteously through the snowbound canyon. "I said that Steele has simply done what any of us would have done had we known the facts."

The discrediting groan from the reporters was audible all the way to the limo. Fitzgerald looked ready to cry. He couldn't think of a single thing to say. Toland hurried through the snow toward him.

"Well, then, where the hell is he?" one of the reporters hollered. "And what was the reward all about, and the cops . . . ? Explain that!"

Toland grabbed the bullhorn roughly. "We were misinformed," he said into the mouthpiece. The echo was awful. He handed the device back to Fitzgerald, cupped his hands around his mouth, and tried to project his flinty voice against the wind. "When our own internal investigation revealed the truth, naturally we understood Mr. Steele's motivation. . . ."

He ignored the cries of "What?," "Speak up!," and "Who is that jerk?!" that flew back at him.

"A motivation," he continued, "that I think you'll all agree is grand, noble—and in complete accord with Ampco's oft-stated goals. . . ."

"What are the police doing here?!"

"What happens to Steele when he gets here?!"

"They give him the Admiral Byrd Award and rename the cereal Frozen Horse Flakes!" someone yelled.

"How'd you find out about this place?" Chris demanded. "Yeah . . . and before God even knew about it!" a shivering reporter added.

Toland's glasses were fogging. "We're publicly stating our apologies to Mr. Steele!" he shouted.

"And we trust that he will continue his highly successful and exciting relationship with Ampco for many years to come!"

"He's setting the horse free, isn't he?" Boyd Templeton, in a WBC parka and Klondike fur cap, called out. He grabbed the bullhorn from Fitzgerald when Toland refused to answer. "You going to try to stop him? That's twelve million dollars' worth of racehorse," Boyd persisted. "How do you think your stockholders are going to feel about that?"

Sears sat rigid in the back seat of the limousine. The windows were sealed and steamed up from the car's heater, but Templeton's voice came through to him with dismaying clarity. Sears adjusted the collar of his topcoat and tugged at his fur-lined leather gloves.

"Sir," Dietrich, who sat beside him, said in a barely audible voice, "I . . . I don't think there's enough food for another night."

Sears' jaw rippled in reply.

"Sir . . ." Dietrich tried again. "I . . . don't think he's coming."

"It's occurred to me," Sears said without turning.

"Do you think . . . I mean, maybe, should we go back to the position that . . ."

"We can't turn around again," the chairman snapped. "Write him off! The Lone Ranger *and* Silver! May they rot in . . ." He leaned forward suddenly and rapped on the soundproof glass partition. "Let's get out of here," he said.

Sonny removed Rising Star's last shoe and offered it ceremoniously to Hallie. She kissed it for luck, then threw it as hard and as far as she could.

"He's calmed down," she said.

Sonny stared off toward the hills. "Until the breeze shifts again."

He took Rising Star's reins and led the horse slowly in the direction of the towering red cliffs. When they got to the stream, Hallie hesitated. The stallion didn't. He plunged through the shallow water and up the verdant bank. Sonny, who'd tried to navigate the rocks carefully, was dripping with water. He hit his hat against his thigh, trying to dry it a bit. Hallie picked her way across the stream, stone by stone, laughing with pleasure and pride at the horse's achievement.

A breeze rustled the tall grass. Rising Star threw back his head and reared. "That's them, all right. And sounds like they've been getting a good scent of you, too," Sonny said, calming the sleek stallion.

Hallie caught up with them. She made a visor of her hand and stared into the sun, stared at the dappled cliffs and hills, hoping for a glimpse of the wild mustangs. Finally, she moved close to Rising Star. She touched his head. It was hard to imagine how terrified of him she had been just yesterday. She patted the thoroughbred's head and stroked his quivering neck. She saw Sonny watching her, smiling.

"We don't go back too far," she whispered to the horse, "but . . . good luck! Never mind that you had a privileged upbringing; you're a *star!* You swing your tail, now," she said. "But don't you forget me!"

She lowered her head and quickly slipped her tinted glasses on. It was hard to see through them. It was hard to see through the sudden blurring of tears. The smell of the horse was on her hand.

She started to wipe it off on her jeans. She started to, but didn't. When he was gone, completely out of sight, she promised herself, then she'd let him go from her. Then she'd wash her hands of him. She stuck her hands in the pockets of her jeans now and watched as best she could with the sun in her eyes and the silly sentimental mist making everything swim softly.

"Excuse us a minute," Sonny said.

She nodded, not trusting herself to speak, and watched as he walked the horse a distance away. Then she took off her glasses and sat down on a rock under a tree to wait.

His words drifted back to her.

"Remember," Sonny told Rising Star, "they're just horses, same as you. Only they never been broke. But they never won no championships, neither. So when you cross that stallion and he wants to fight, you just remember, you got the blood on your side."

"Will he go?" Hallie called out. "Just like that?"

"You bet."

"But . . . I thought you guys were pals."

Sonny took off the horse's bridle. Rising Star shook his dark handsome mane and reared again, as if with the thrill, the nearness and newness, of freedom. "We are pals," Sonny said. Then he turned back to Rising Star. "Go get 'em, junkie!" He swatted the horse hard on the flanks. Rising Star turned and galloped away. "Make something out of yourself, now," Sonny called after him softly.

Hallie waited a moment, then got up and joined him. They stood there for quite a long time. They waited until the last bit of dust settled in the stallion's wake, until he was a dark form moving nimbly along a ridge of red rocks, until there was nothing but the wind and the sound of wild mustangs calling in their strangely urgent voices through the peaceful canyon.

"What now?"

"Let's get a cup of coffee," he said. He put his arm around her and they started walking again. They walked to the edge of the stream.

"Wait," Hallie said. She knelt and washed her hands in the icy mountain water. Then she shook them dry and made her way back across the stones. Sonny followed and caught up with her on the other side. He picked up his saddle and blanket roll. They walked along together to the opening in the rocks, through the pass. They walked until they got to the highway.

"Isn't that heavy?" Hallie asked him, nodding at the saddle.

"Been carrying it all my life."

She smiled. "Which way's the coffee?"

He pretended to sniff the breeze. "Believe it's down wind," he said.

They leaned against one another wearily, then continued along the gravelly edge of the road. They didn't speak again until they got to a tiny town. The café served as the local bus depot.

"Everything nice and convenient, just the way I ordered it," Sonny said.

He pushed the door open for her. They didn't bother about dark glasses anymore. Sonny took a seat at a front table and stared out at a small boy who was washing the window. Hallie phoned New York. When she got back to the table, her coffee was waiting. The saucer was on top of the cup.

"Kept it warm for you."

"Thanks."

"Bus is on time, they say."

"Which bus?"

"Bus that'll get you to the airport. They don't have no rent-a-cars in this town."

"Oh?" She took a sip of coffee. "How do you feel?"

"Good," he said. "Maybe not as good as him, but good. . . . What'd they say—your boss and all?"

"Oh, you know . . . lots of congratulations . . . can't wait to get the story, particularly with Ampco reversing their position."

He laughed. "I bet."

"They have me going to Paris next . . . covering the elections."

"No kidding? That'd be interesting."

She was staring down glumly at the muddy coffee when the waitress arrived with a fresh pot, and a doughnut with an candle stuck in it. "More coffee?" the woman asked.

"No . . . no, thanks," Hallie said.

"Yes, thank you," said Sonny.

"Well, all right. I guess so," Hallie said. Then she saw the doughnut. The waitress set it down in front of her.

Sonny leaned over and lit the candle. "A little something for the road," he said.

Hallie laughed. "God . . . ! Would I love to see *you* in Paris!"

Sonny laughed with her. "Yeah! Me and them guys with the gold chains 'round their necks in them fancy restaurants. We'd have lots to say to each other!"

Their laughter faded into soft smiles. They looked at each other. Then Sonny turned away. He pointed to a spot on the window that the boy had missed. The kid nodded and went for it industriously.

"Want something to read? A magazine or something?" he asked her.

"No, thanks." She reached across to get the cream and her sleeve landed in a melting pat of butter. Sonny took her wrist.

"Careful," he said. He dipped his napkin into a glass of water and began cleaning off the butter spot.

Hallie watched him silently. Then, while he worked on her sleeve, she said, "Now, tell the truth, Norm. Did you ever think it would be this tough to lose a pain in the ass like me?"

He stopped, looked at her, then replied levelly, "Had no idea."

The P.A. system crackled through the little café: "'Board for Las Vegas, Los Angeles, San Diego!"

"That's you," Sonny said. "Listen here. I've been thinking . . . I got something I'd like you to have, just for a souvenir." He reached down into his saddlebags.

"If it's another candlelit jelly doughnut, you sure picked a hell of a place to hide it!"

"Ain't," he said, grinning. He pulled a piece of faded blue fabric out of his bag. It was a workshirt, or had been, Hallie realized. Now it was the bedraggled gift-wrapping for the "souvenir" he was giving her. He stuck the balled-up old denim shirt into her tote bag. "Open it later," he said. "Come on. Coffee and doughnut's on me." They walked toward the door. "Listen . . . this story you're going to tell . . . be nice if you didn't mention where we let him go."

"Silver Reef?? Leave out a name like that?"

He sighed and shook his head.

"You know, there's a lot more to New York than 'Bloomingburg's' or those 'Madison Square Gardens'. It's a wonderful city, honest. Have you ever seen it? I mean *really* seen it?"

"You're flirting, Alice," he said.

"Maybe."

"Besides, I don't see you in a trailer, making sure there's enough cold beer. . . . Bet you can't even find where the quarter goes in the laundromat."

"You're flirting, Norman."

"You'd run out on me in a month's time."

She caught his eye, then nodded. "Probably," she said.

There were a few people standing in line as the driver opened the bus door. Beyond the bus and the little town, Hallie saw the mountains rearing clean and crisp against the late afternoon sky. "Hard to believe you won't . . . you and Rising Star won't be there in the morning," she said.

"You're going to miss that animal, huh?"

She looked directly at him. Her heart plummeted suddenly, fell into the churning emptiness of her gut. "Yes," she said. "I wonder where he'll be tonight." She managed a shaky smile. "I hope she's good enough for him."

"Oh, she's good enough, all right."

She didn't ask how he knew. "What'll you do tomorrow, Sonny?"

"Get moving on," he said. "Something simple . . . hard, maybe . . . but plain, quiet."

All the passengers but Hallie were on the bus. "Well, you've still got my card?"

He nodded. "Still got it. Don't need it though,

do I? All I've got to do is switch on the news. You'll be there, won't you?"

"Right at the top of the ratings."

He handed her bag to her. "Hey," he called as she started up the steps, "I . . . keep wanting to thank you, but then I keep wondering what for."

She smiled quickly. "I know! Me, too!"

They grinned at each other then. "Maybe for how I'm going to feel whenever I see your face on the TV," he said. "Guess I'm going to have to get me a TV."

"I know how I'm going to feel when I hear the word 'cowboy.'" She turned quickly, then turned back. "So you won't forget me entirely?"

"Not entirely," he said softly.

"Ready, ma'am?" the bus driver called.

Sonny cupped her chin in his hand and kissed her. She felt a wetness on her lips that she thought was his. Maybe it was, but the taste of tears mingled with it quickly and she was horrified because she thought she'd never be sure now. She breathed in deeply. She breathed in the scent and taste and memory, the softness of his lips. She drew back.

"So long, Alice," he whispered into her ear.

"So long, Norman."

He stepped away from the door. "You have a safe trip back, now."

She didn't feel like looking at his gift immediately. She thought there would be a right time for it and that she'd know instinctively when it was. She allowed herself to reach into her bag and just hold onto the shirt, however. She held it and stared out the window of the bus and watched the countryside they'd traveled on foot move by in a flash. It felt like someone was rewinding her life, reversing the picture, making it all go backward too quickly. She needed to slow it down, make it last a little longer yet.

She let go of the shirt and took out of her purse the pages she had scrawled. She put on her glasses and pulled a cigarette from the bottom of her bag and chewed on the unlit filter end of it. When she'd finished rereading what she'd written on the mountain, she dug into her bag again for some fresh paper. It was getting dark out. She took one last look at the land outside softening in the early twilight. Then she switched on the overhead light and went to work.

There was no doubt that Sonny Steele would get what he wanted now. What he wanted was anonymity, for a while. Privacy. To disappear. To find, on his own, in his own sweet time, what Wendell Hixson had called "the best part of himself."

She began to write. By the time the bus pulled into the depot, she'd outlined most of the story. She'd even written an epilogue to it:

*So ends the bizarre saga of horse-racing's most honored stallion, and the unusual man who set him free . . . except for a minor postscript. Mr. Steele will be happy to hear that his name is not as well known as it was— even a week ago. Signs fade, other faces get pasted over. You'll have your privacy back, Sonny. Your "self." I wish I were around to see you smile at not being recognized. I wish I were around . . . just to make a little trouble.*

*There's no place I'll ever be that I won't— for just one moment—see with your eyes . . . the way I saw those beautiful high places,*

*that canyon without a name, where Rising
Star's running now. And . . . and the way you
showed me . . . me. I envy the people you
talked to this morning, somewhere down the
road. Where was it? Some dusty café where
they serve candlelit doughnuts?*

*I miss you, cowboy, and hope to see you
again one day. For now . . . forever . . . wherever you are, good luck, Sonny. I hope this
finds you . . . well.*

The bus stopped. The aisle lights went on.
Through the window, she saw a limousine waiting.
The driver was holding a sign with her name
printed on it. She grabbed her bag and hurried
off the bus.

"Miss Martin?"

"That's me."

He opened the back door of the limo and she
tossed in her tote. She was still holding onto the
pages she'd written. She knew she'd never get
away with the epilogue. She was too good a reporter to get . . . personal. She was too good an
editor not to delete the whole damned postscript.

"Mr. Charles said for me to get you some good
champagne," the driver said, "the best they had
in the store. But I didn't know that this was a dry
county till I got here. I'm very sorry, Miss Martin.
I got you some Champale, though. Pink Champale.
We can get some real champagne just over the
line, on the way to the airport."

"Fine," Hallie said. She climbed into the plush-
velvet back seat and took the bottle of Champale
out of the ice bucket. She looked at it and then at
the pages in her hand and she began to laugh.
And then, all of a sudden, she wanted to cry.

It was time, she decided. But first she separated the final pages from the rest of the story and tore them up. She opened the little bottle of malt liquor and poured herself a glass. Then she pulled out the shirt. She unwrapped it carefully. Inside was Sonny Steele's silver belt buckle. A winner's buckle; a champion's reward.

"Miss Martin," the driver called to her. He opened the glass partition. "I'm sorry. I almost forgot. Mr. Charles said to tell you that they're shining up an Emmy for you. . . ."

Hallie smiled. "He's too late," she said. "Someone beat him to it. A cowboy!"

"Sonny Steele?" the man guessed.

"Who?"

"You know, the breakfast-food cowboy. Aren't you the one who . . ."

"*That* Sonny Steele? No, it wasn't him."

He looked disappointed. He shrugged and closed the partition.

Hallie took off her boots and wriggled her toes. All things considered, she figured, her toes had survived better than she'd expected they would. They looked kind of cramped and put upon. The nail polish on them was chipped and ragged. She looked at her fingernails. The polish on them had just about worn away, too. Raggedy-assed nails for the rugged individualist.

Suddenly she remembered how Sonny had removed Rising Star's horseshoes in Silver Reef Canyon. She remembered that he had given the last shoe to her; the last vestige of any man's claim on the stallion; the last obstacle to total freedom. She banged on the glass partition. The driver pressed the button and the glass descended again.

"Stop, please."

"Here . . . ? There's nothing here, Miss Martin. Just the mountains. It's real cold out there now."

"It will only take a minute. Please."

"You're the boss," he said skeptically. He slowed, then stopped the car on the shoulder of the highway.

Hallie rolled down her window. She picked up her muddied boots, all two hundred forty-five dollars' worth of soft Italian leather, and hurled them into the darkness. "Good luck, junkie," she whispered. "Thank you, Norman."

# 15.

# EPILOGUE WITHOUT
# A POSTSCRIPT

Wendell signaled for another beer. The little road-house was empty except for the Greyhound passengers, the lady bartender, and a tired waitress. Behind the bar, a grainy black-and-white television set was on. The sound was turned down low.

Leroy returned from the men's room. He'd washed his face and slicked back his black hair, but he still looked sleepy and rumpled from the ride. "Make that two," he told the barmaid. "Lord, how much farther we got to go tonight?"

"Ranch's another couple hours away yet," Wendell said.

"Let me see that letter."

"Threw it away."

"Why? How come you did that?"

" 'Dear Wendell and Leroy,' " Wendell recited from memory. " 'Okay, I done it now. I hope you ain't too mad at me. I did what I had to do. With love and affection, I remain . . .'"

"He 'remains'! What do *we* remain?" Leroy shook his head.

"Sonny done us a favor, Lee." Wendell tossed some change on the bar and took a long swallow of the frosty beer. "Been so long since we talked about *now. Any* of us. 'Did, did, was, was'—remember, Sonny used to say that. 'Who rode Bubbles and who throwed Twinkles . . . remember this, remember that.'"

"Yeah, he sure brought us up to date now, all right! Back to Leo Marston's ranch. Probably still runs it like a damned concentration camp!"

Wendell turned and looked outside. It was dark and windy and night clouds rode across the face of the moon. "Nice out there," he said softly. "Not a single building high enough to hide the moon. Not a blinking electrical sign or neon light fightin' the stars. . . ."

"Don't you wonder where he is?"

"No," Wendell said.

"How come . . . everybody always paid so much attention to Sonny?"

Wendell tossed his head to free the iron-gray ponytail that was lodged between his shirt and jacket collar. Then he shrugged. "He's just . . . one of them guys people like to pay attention to."

"Guess you don't have to hide your hair no more." Leroy grinned.

"Never did!"

"You telling me you *liked* tucking it under your shirt that way?!"

"Myra, come here," the barmaid called to the waitress. "They're talking about that cowboy of yours. . . ."

"Sonny Steele?" The tired woman came back to life. She hurried to the bar. "He ain't 'my cowboy,' no ways. . . . Ooooh, but a gal can dream! They got his picture on again?"

"Hey . . . excuse me, ma'am!" Wendell hollered to the barmaid. "Think you could turn that up a mite? Leroy, it's her. It's that reporter who took off after him."

"Damn," Leroy said. "There she is, sure enough! The one what liked my ring!"

"Hey, good buddies, puh-lease!" the waitress said.

"You all better hush up around Myra when Mr. Sonny Steele's name comes on the television set," her friend teased.

On the screen of the little black-and-white TV, Hallie sat behind a long curved desk. Boyd Templeton was visible for a moment to her right. Then the camera moved in for a closeup.

". . . all charges have been dropped and, according to one company source, the Ampco art department is hard at work designing a new logo. . . ."

"Wonder if they're accepting suggestions," Leroy said.

"What you got in mind?"

Leroy winked at the waitress, who was glaring at him. "Couldn't say . . . what with ladies present. But if Leo Marston's still rearing bulls, they'll be plenty of it where we're going!"

"As to the whereabouts of Rising Star," Hallie said. She paused. Wendell leaned across the bar, transfixed. "Nothing further is known." Hallie began to gather up her papers.

"Shoot!" Wendell said. "She knows! Did you see her face? That little lady knows right where Sonny stashed that racehorse! I told you I liked her eyes, didn't I?"

"So ends the bizarre saga of horse-racing's most honored stallion . . . and the man who set him free." Hallie looked directly into the camera now. "Except for a final note of thanks from this reporter to Mr. Steele for his . . . cooperation in bringing this story to you. . . ."

"I'll be damned," Wendell said.

The barmaid shushed him this time.

"Wherever he is at this moment," Hallie continued, "I'm sure I speak on behalf of our viewers in saying, Good luck, cowboy. I hope this finds you . . . well."

"Amen," said the waitess.

"This is Hallie Martin in New York . . . saying good night."

"What you'll be damned?" Leroy wanted to know.

"That gal . . . she's sweet on Sonny."

"Go on!"

Wendell took another sip of his beer and grinned broadly. "Ladies love outlaws, Leroy. It's a fact."

"How come you all know so much about that cowboy?" the waitress said. She'd taken her lipstick out of her apron pocket and was putting it on, watching herself in the mirror behind the bar.

"What made you say a fool thing like that?" Leroy asked.

Wendell shrugged. "Never mind." He finished off the beer. "Princes and fools. Watchers and doers," he muttered.

The barmaid lowered the volume on the TV again, smoothed her blouse over her wide double-knit hips, and sauntered toward Wendell. The waitress ran her tongue across her freshly pearlized pink lips. "You know, he done something . . . great . . . that Sonny Steele! He surely did."

"Oh, yeah? What's that?" Leroy asked.

The waitress named Myra laughed. "I don't know. But he did . . . didn't he, Doris?"

"What you think?" the barmaid asked Wendell.

"He was always a champion. Born and bred to win."

"Probably had the best of everything," the waitress said.

Leroy stared hard at the woman. His brow furrowed in concentration . . . remembering . . . trying to remember. He had one of those strange feelings, as if he'd lived through this exact moment before.

*Déjà vu.*

Then it came to him. A night in a hotel suite somewhere, during their last swing through the Southwest. The horse's picture had come on the television screen. Sonny was all bent out of shape with pain.

"Born to win," he'd said about the horse. "Born and bred a champion."

"Probably had the best of everything," he'd told Sonny.

"Probably never drew a free breath yet," Sonny had said.

Leroy whirled suddenly. "I know why he done it, Wendell! I know now!"

Wendell smiled and nodded his head.

Leroy finished off his beer. "You remember that time up in Calgary when Sonny drew that bull?"

"Cochese!" Wendell snapped his fingers, remembering.

"Rode him for three seconds!!"

Leroy shook his head and laughed. "Didn't even make day money on that one."

The waitress cleared her throat and put a hand to her hair, which was orange and piled in chaotic curls on top of her head. "I *said* . . ." She pouted prettily at Leroy. "How come you all know so much about Sonny Steele?"

Leroy looked her over, then turned to Wendell. The barmaid was resting her chin on her hands, staring at the bearded cowboy's cool blue eyes. Leroy glanced questioningly at him.

Wendell pushed his glass toward the plump and shapely woman. "Fill 'er up again, sweet thing, would you?" Then he winked at Leroy. "Tell the gal, Lee," he said. "Wasn't you and Sonny . . ."— he crossed his fingers—". . . just like that?!"